A Little Bit Witchy

Riddler's Edge Book One

by A.A. Albright

This is a work of fiction. Names, characters, organisations, places, events and incidents are either products of the author's imagination, or are used fictitiously.

Mailing List: http://www.subscribepage.com/z4n0f4
Website: https://aaalbright.com

Chapters

1. The Daily Dubliner

2. Let's Go Round the Bend

3. Life Is But A Dream

4. There Has Most Definitely *Not* Been a Murder on the Riddler's Express

5. The Vander Inn

6. The Daily Riddler

7. Undying Love

8. Norman Normal

9. To the Lighthouse

10. Can't See the Woods for the Mist

11. Riddler's Cove

12. Fuzz

13. The Evening Edition

14. Fish Fingers

15. Wizardly Wagon

16. Rat in a Cage

17. The Best Man for the Job

18. The Fisherman's Friend

19. Family Ties

20. The Sweet, Sweet Taste of Crud

21. The Kiss of Life

22. The Things We Do For Love

23. The Test

24. A Little Bit Witchy

Extract from the Compendium of Supernatural Beings

1. The Daily Dubliner

I sat in the most uncomfortable chair in the world, staring at my computer screen.

Bike for sale in Blanchardstown. Seat, handlebars and back wheel missing, otherwise in good nick. Call after six.

Cat bed for sale. 10 euro if you want the cat sick washed off, 5 euro if unwashed. Call at any time.

Wild pigeons for sale. Meet me on O'Connell Street to discuss terms.

I banged my head against my desk. Was this *really* what my life had come to? A few short months ago I had been a reporter on this very newspaper. I was going places. Now … now I was stuck in the basement of the Daily Dubliner office, preparing classified advertisements and obituaries.

The rest of the morning went on much the same. A woman wanted to sell all of her old shoes, and made sure to add that only the left one of each pair smelled like cheese. A band was looking for a new singer, who had to look like a supermodel and sing like a siren. A modelling agency was looking for new models – and would only charge a three hundred euro fee for a consultation. What a bargain.

As the phone rang for the umpteenth time, I decided to bang my head on my desk again – might as well get the frustration out before I had to talk to the latest nutter – and picked up the receiver.

'Daily Dubliner classified ads,' I said. 'Aisling Smith speaking. How may I help you?'

The person on the other end seemed to be hacking up phlegm. After a few seconds, he said, 'Got a room for rent. Lupin Lane. Three twenty a month.'

My heart began to drum, and I pulled my special notebook towards me, frantically scribbling.

'Lupin Lane,' I said. 'Where *is* that exactly?'

The caller hacked a bit more phlegm and said, 'Y'know. If you know, you know.'

'Yes,' I said. 'But I don't know. Tell you what – I'll let you include full directions at no extra charge. You'll get a lot more potential renters that way.'

He hacked, and then (I think) he spat. Finally, he said, 'Nah. You're all right doll.' He went on to quickly list his credit card details and phone number, not letting me get another word in before he finally hung up.

I stabbed my notebook page with my pen a few times, muttered, 'Criminy, criminy, criminy!' and then reluctantly prepared the advertisement.

That was the tenth weird address this week alone, I thought, as I read over the details in my special notebook. And the third occurrence of Lupin Lane. I flipped through the pages I'd filled so far. There were rooms for rent and items for sale in Madra Lane, Lupin Lane, Westerly Crescent, and quite a few more places that didn't actually exist.

I was making some notes in the margins, trying to make sense of it all, when a shadow fell across my desk – a short, oddly-shaped shadow which belonged to the paper's editor.

'Hey John.' I covered up my notebook. 'How em … how can I help you?'

'I saw you hide a notebook, Ash,' he said. 'Show it to me.'

I picked up my coffee, taking a casual slug. 'Ugh! Cold!' I shuddered and pushed the cup away. 'You look nice today, John.'

Remind me, will you, that the next time I tell a lie, I ought to make it less obvious. John did not look nice. John never looked nice. And it had nothing to do with the fact that he was short, round and bald. There were lots of bald guys I fancied. Bruce Willis. Mark Strong. Okay, so that was just two. But still.

'Thanks,' he said, puffing up his chest. 'I'm on a new diet. I can eat anything I like as long as it's meat.'

'Ah.' I nodded, taking another sip of my cold coffee. Sure, it was disgusting – but at least I could pretend that the grimace on my face was caused by the beverage. 'That sounds great. You can really tell. Hey, em ... how's it all going up above? Anything you guys need help with?'

He sat down on top of my desk, crossing his legs and picking up one of my pens. It had a bobbly unicorn on top, and he started to wave it back and forth. 'You really like unicorns, don't you? I don't know many other thirty-year-old women who do.'

'I'm twenty-nine, actually,' I informed him. The truth was I *could* have been thirty. I really had no idea of my precise age – but I'll tell you more about that in a while. For now, all you need to know is that, whether John was wrong or John was right, he just had the sort of face that I was *always* going to disagree with.

'Sure.' He smirked. 'Because that really makes a difference. You know, my little niece likes unicorns, too. She's three. Oh, and in answer to your question – no. There is *nothing* you can get involved in up above. Now show me the notebook.'

Darn it! I was sure I'd managed to distract him. 'Oh, I don't have a notebook,' I said vaguely. 'You must have imagined it. Hey, are you sure you're getting enough calories on this diet of yours? Last time I went on a cleanse I started to hallucinate. I was totally convinced that the woman in the spa was a vampire. True story.'

For a moment he just looked at me, arms crossed across his large upper body, forehead sweating as his anger increased. As you can see, the feeling of loathing I felt towards my boss was *very* much reciprocated. After looking at me for a few seconds more, he lunged across my desk, grabbed the notebook and said, 'Aha! I knew you were up to something.'

I stood up, towering over him even though I was an average five foot six and wearing flat-heeled shoes. 'You can't open that, John. It's an invasion of privacy!'

He wriggled out of my reach and sped away from the desk. How did he move so quickly? He was like a cat, I tell you. And not one of the cute, fluffy ones. He was more like one of those sneaky, stinky cats who manage to poop in corners without you ever catching them.

'You don't *have* any privacy while you're at work, Ash.' He was at the other side of the room now, standing under the small window, opening my notebook and peering at the pages. 'What *is* this? Why are you writing out all of these classified ads?'

My brain raced to come up with an excuse. 'As a hard copy. I mean – duh. In case the computer system goes down.'

'Uh huh,' he said, sounding about as convinced as he ought to be. 'So what's with the notes in the margins, then? *"Madra Lane – could this be an illegal puppy farm?"* What the ...?'

I ran across the room and snatched the notebook from his hands. 'You're a terrible boss, do you know that?'

He sniggered. 'Oh, don't say that. You're breaking my heart.' He crossed back to my desk and made himself uncomfortable in my chair, then began to paw through all of my paperwork. 'I knew you were up to something down here. I just knew it. You couldn't just work out your probationary period like a normal person, could you? You're back to your old conspiracy theory nonsense again.'

I looked away from him. As editors go, I really wished he would – go somewhere, anywhere else, as long as it was far away from me. 'It's not conspiracy nonsense,' I said testily, crossing my arms. 'It was *never* conspiracy nonsense. I'm making notes of place names in our classifieds section. Places that don't actually exist. I think it could be code used by criminal gangs. Madra is Irish for dog, which is what made me think that Madra Lane could refer to an illegal puppy farm.'

'Criminal gangs!' he said with a sneer. 'Criminal *gangs*! Ash, there are new housing developments going up all over Dublin, all the time. Just because you haven't heard of a place doesn't mean it doesn't exist.'

He sat back, looking smug. He seemed to think he'd just said the smartest thing in the world.

'I don't assume that because I've never heard of a place it doesn't exist,' I said. 'I *know* these places don't exist because I've looked into it. Extensively. These addresses are not registered. These addresses do *not* exist.'

He kicked his chubby little legs up on my desk. 'You know what went through my mind when I woke up this morning? I lay there in my bed, and I thought – I'm going to go and check on Ash today. Gonna take a trip downstairs and see how well she's doing with her probation. If she's being a model employee, I thought, then I *might* let her write some stories again. Within certain parameters, obviously. But if she's up to any of her old tricks, I thought – seeing things where there's nothing to be seen, wasting the newspaper's time and money on wild goose chases – well then, I'm finally going to do what I've dreamt of doing since the day I met Aisling Smith. I'm going to fire her.'

I glared at him. I felt like hacking up some phlegm of my own – preferably in his direction. Not only had he told me he was about to fire me. He'd also slipped the disturbing image of him lying in bed into the mix. The dastardly knave. Now I was going to need to come up with some way of washing that picture out of my brain.

'Fire me, then,' I said, with about as much bravado as a rabbit at the end of a farmer's gun. 'There are a dozen other papers who'd love to have me on board. And as an investigative journalist, I might add. You know – that thing that I'm actually qualified to do.'

Sure, I thought. There were lots of papers hiring right now. Because print news was doing *so* well. Still, the Daily Dubliner was selling a decent amount of copies, so maybe John thought all papers were the same. He did seem like the self-involved sort.

He sniggered for a few minutes. Then he picked up my unicorn pen again, and used it to scratch his armpit. As he finished off, and moved the pen across his chest, I gasped. 'You ... you … you put my pen down right now. Do *not* scratch your other armpit!'

He looked straight at me, and scratched.

Oh, the humanity. Or … the unicornity. Whatever it was called, it was a travesty.

'Here,' he said with a grin, holding the pen towards me. 'I'm finished with it now. You can have it back.'

Oh, how I wanted to take that poor pen out of his hands and give it a decent burial. But much as I loved it, it was tainted now. And possibly carrying a few communicable diseases, as well.

'You can keep it,' I said, grabbing my bag and stalking across the floor.

For a moment he didn't react – probably because he was too busy using the poor pen to scratch the inside of one of his ears. But once he'd waxed it up good and proper, he wobbled out of the chair and raced after me. 'Hey!' he called out. 'Where do you think you're going?'

I paused at the staircase. 'Oh, I don't know,' I said. 'Maybe for an early lunch. I mean, I can do what I like now, can't I? Seeing as you've fired the best journalist you've ever had.'

His eyes bulged, and he clapped a hand over his mouth, struggling to hold his laughter inside. 'Okay, let's set your incredible ego aside for a moment. I didn't say you *were* fired. I said I was *going* to fire you. And as much as I'd still like to do that, I don't own this newspaper.'

I felt my nose scrunch up. Partially because he had just begun to chew my wax-covered, disease-ridden pen, and partially because I was confused. 'Wait … what are you saying? I'm *not* fired?'

He shrugged. 'I mean, if you've got better job offers – which I highly doubt – then you're free to go. But no, unfortunately you're not fired. The old man wants to have lunch with you today. And for reasons I will *never* understand, he actually wants to offer you a trial position that could lead to a promotion *and* a pay rise.'

My lashes were going a bit fluttery, what with all of the shock. I did my best to compose myself, and tossed my hair. 'Oh. Well, of course he does. Why wouldn't he?'

2. Let's Go Round the Bend

As I walked to Capel Street, I tried to recall what little I knew of Arnold Albright. I'd only met him twice – once, when he bought the newspaper last July, and again when he briefly attended the staff Christmas party. He had white hair, pale blue eyes, and carried a cane everywhere he went. He seemed like your average sweet old man. But your average sweet old man didn't own a newspaper – *many* newspapers, according to John. Behind that innocent smile he'd worn, I'd sensed something shrewd.

As I neared the café, one of my migraines began to come on. I say migraines because that's what the doctor called them. There was no headache, just an odd blurring of my vision, like I was looking at the world through a hazy kaleidoscope. Ten separate tests told me I had perfect eyesight, so I had no choice but to accept my doc's diagnosis.

The thing about these migraines, though, was that they were oddly specific. Take that very moment, for instance. The café, called *Let's Go Round the Bend,* looked perfectly normal to me. As did the shop next door to it – an antique place called *Times of Yore.* But the drainpipe *between* the two exteriors. Now, that was shimmering.

I shook my head and looked again. Yep, the drainpipe was still shimmering. Not only was it shimmering, but I could have sworn a guy just walked out *through* the drainpipe.

'Get it together, Ash,' I muttered. 'It's nerves, that's all it is. You need to believe in yourself. You deserve a better job.'

I wasn't so sure John would agree.

I took a deep breath, crossed the road, and entered *Let's Go Round the Bend.* Although I was early, Arnold was already there, sitting at a table by the window. I took a seat across from him, taking him in – he was wearing gold, round-rimmed eyeglasses. He had his usual cane with him – it looked hand-carved, with a golden spiral running along the wood. He had been reading from a small, spiral-bound notebook, but he closed it as soon as I entered and smiled up at me.

'Miss Smith,' he said warmly. 'Forgive me for not standing up to greet you. I have age-appropriate hips.'

I laughed a little, and sat down across from him.

'I took the liberty of ordering,' he went on. 'I hope you don't mind. But I did make sure it was your favourite – minestrone soup.' He pushed a cup of coffee towards me. 'And I got you a drink, too.'

'Thank you,' I said. 'But how did you know I liked minestrone?'

He patted his nose. 'I've been a newspaperman all my life, Miss Smith. I make it my business to know everything about the people who work for me. After all, it's a serious business, a newspaper. Say a group of armed men took over some government or other right now. Why, one paper could report that they were rebels, fighting for their freedom. Another could paint them as terrorists, and a scourge to be destroyed. I like to know if my writers have agendas.'

The waitress arrived with our food. Arnold seemed to have ordered the minestrone for himself as well. I waited until it was all laid out before replying. 'Sure,' I said. 'I agree that it's important to know who's working for you. Although it's usually the owners of media companies who get to spin the narrative, not the lowly journalists. And also – I doubt my taste in soup tells you an awful lot about me other than the fact that I like smoked paprika.'

He paused, his spoon halfway to his mouth. 'You'd be surprised, Miss Smith. It tells me a lot, in fact. It tells me that you have the same favourite soup as me. It was my daughter's favourite, too.'

'Oh. Well … that's good to know,' I said, beginning to eat. I mean, I suppose it wasn't the strangest conversation I'd had that week. It *definitely* wasn't the strangest conversation I'd had that day. But just because it wasn't the strangest didn't mean it wasn't strange.

We ate in silence for a few minutes. The soup was delicious, nicer than any minestrone I'd ever had. As I scraped the last of it from my bowl, I said, 'The food's great here. You chose a good place.'

'Oh?' His brows shot up to his hairline. 'You like it? You feel … comfortable … here?'

'Of course I do. Who wouldn't? I'm going to add it to my list of great places to eat.'

'Oh, that does make me happy.' He smiled, sitting back as the waitress collected our bowls. 'I've ordered Mississippi mud pie for dessert.'

Wow, he really had been doing his research. Favourite soup. Favourite dessert. Any moment now he was going to start listing off David Bowie songs. As nice as it was that he'd made an effort to find out about me, I was wondering when he was going to start talking about the job.

'You grew up in the system, I believe,' he said, sipping his coffee. 'And you were placed with quite a lot of foster families over the years.'

It took me a moment to calm my thoughts down, let alone even think about replying. 'So is that why you're considering me for this mysterious new job, then?' I asked. 'It's a charity thing? Because I have to tell you, Mr Albright, I don't need anyone's charity. I've managed quite all right on my own for the past twenty-nine years.'

My voice was shaking, and my hands too, so I can see why you *might* be thinking I have a few unresolved childhood issues.

'Forgive me. I didn't mean to be insensitive,' he said. 'It's the reporter in me, you see. I always found the human interest aspect the most worthwhile to write about. Something the readers can relate to. And your story is particularly fascinating. You were left in front of a hospital, I believe. You were almost two at the time – although that's only an educated guess on the doctors' behalves. You *could* be twenty-nine. It seems like the safest estimate. But you could also be twenty-eight, or thirty ... I wonder, have you ever tried to trace the woman who abandoned you?'

I pulled the sugar and milk towards me, spilling a liberal amount of each into my coffee. I didn't actually *like* sugar or milk in my coffee, but I didn't need to drink it, I just needed something to do while I tried to keep my cool. 'No. I've never tried to trace her.'

His head tilted to the side and he looked intently at me. 'Really? How fascinating. I've read your work, Miss Smith. Your journalistic instinct is clearly strong, and yet you've resisted solving *this* mystery. Why, you don't even know your real date of birth. Nor your actual name.'

Was I really going to keep sitting here, I wondered? Either this man wanted a pet project, or he was seriously sadistic. Either way, I didn't think he was a man I wanted to know. 'I do know my name. My mother – or whoever abandoned me – left a note around my neck. It said, "This is my little girl. Her name is Aisling. Please make sure she knows I love her very much."' As I spoke, I kept my voice as steady as I could.

'Ah, yes.' He nodded. 'Aisling. The name means *vision.* A beautiful name. I couldn't have chosen better myself, given the chance.'

I took a sip of the sweet, milky coffee, trying not to gag. 'John said it ought to mean visions of the impending apocalypse.'

'Yes. John does seem to have taken a bit of a dislike to you. He has you working in the basement, I believe. Arranging the classified ads, the death notices, that sort of thing.'

I took another sip. 'Oh. You know about that. Well then …'

He smiled up at the waitress for a moment, as she set our desserts down. 'Could you bring us some more coffee, my dear? My guest has accidentally poured milk and sugar into hers, and she's having a bit of trouble keeping it down.' He turned back to me. 'Why am I offering you a chance at this promotion? Well, it's quite simple.

I've been following your work.' He opened the notebook, and pulled out some folded-up news articles. 'Read this one out to me, would you?' He passed the first article my way.

As I looked down at it, I gulped. Yes, it was one of mine all right. The last one, in fact, that John had let me write.

Dublin: City of Vice or City of Vampires?

Last night, while taking a shortcut through an alley off Bachelors Walk, a young woman was viciously attacked. Luckily, the attacker was disturbed by a crowd of people journeying down the same alley. She has yet to be caught.

Yes, you read that right, folks. Alison Shannon was attacked by another young woman, a woman who Alison described as, 'Stunningly beautiful, in a Transylvanian sort of way. Wearing a lot of eyeliner and dark lipstick.'

Alison is now recovering at home, feeling very weak. She told this reporter, 'I swear she was trying to take a bite out of my neck. I think she might have been a vampire.'

I read the article aloud, keeping my eyes on the page, terrified to see Arnold's reaction. John had laughed his socks off when I submitted this one. Well, actually, he hadn't been wearing socks that day (I guess he felt like stinking his shoes out even more than usual) but if he *had* been wearing them, he would have laughed them off.

When I finished reading, Arnold passed me the second article. 'And this,' he said, 'is the same article with John's edits. Would you please read it aloud?'

Holding back a sigh, I read John's version.

Last night, while taking a shortcut through an alley off Bachelors Walk, a young woman was almost mugged. Luckily, the would-be mugger was disturbed by a crowd of people journeying down the same alley.

The mugger was most likely a drug-addict, looking for money for the next fix. The suspect has not yet been caught.

I finally looked at Arnold. His expression was completely blank. 'Are you going to say the same as John, then? That my story was ridiculous? Because as much as I want to impress you today, I'm not going to agree with John's opinion. My story was not ridiculous. My story was exactly what journalism should be. It was the full, unbiased truth.'

He didn't say anything for a moment. He was quickly leafing through the little notebook, his lips moving slightly as he read. 'John gave you ten written warnings before he moved you to the basement, I believe,' he said eventually. 'There was the time when you reported that a woman saw a wolf in her front garden. John asked you to change wolf into *big dog,* you argued your point, and he issued you with a warning. There was another instance where you reported that a security guard on his way home through the Phoenix Park had seen a Golden Labrador change into a man. Again, John felt the need to edit your article.' He laughed. 'I believe that in one of his reports to me, John suggested you might be better off writing fantasy novels.'

I felt my face redden as he listed off more of the stories I'd submitted to John. 'Well, when you read them all out like that, I can see why it appears there's a bit of a pattern,' I said. 'But I stand by what I said to you a moment ago. I was reporting the facts. I was *doing* my job.'

He closed the notebook, crossing his palms and placing them on top, his eyes looking steadily at mine. 'It's clear that you've been reporting nothing other than what you've been told,' he said. 'But … do *you* ever see these kinds of things? Vampires, werewolves and the like?'

My second cup of coffee had arrived, and I picked the sugar up and began to pour. Stuff him, anyway. He didn't know everything about me. I could grow to like sugar in my coffee. In fact, I was going to *make* myself like sugar in my coffee just to spite him.

'I see what this is now,' I said. 'You're a rich old man, and you want to make some sort of a difference before you die. You want to help people – people you think are pathetic, like me.' I furiously stirred the coffee, the spoon clanging loudly against the cup. 'Well, I'm not pathetic, thank you very much,' I said, standing up and gathering up my things. 'I don't need you to offer me a new position in your empire just because you feel sorry for me. Or because you think I have mental health issues. Which I do *not.* I don't see vampires, or werewolves, or whatever else you said. I've told you before and I'll tell you again. I'm a reporter. Therefore, I report.'

Okay, so I *had* been convinced I saw a vampire at the spa that one time. But like I told John, I was doing a cleanse. I'd had nothing but cucumber water for that entire day.

'Please,' Arnold said, reaching out for my hand. 'This is nothing like that. I apologise once again. I never should have brought your past into things. Will you sit back down?'

I eyed him warily. I still couldn't shake the feeling that I was this man's pet project, but dignity didn't pay the rent. Reluctantly, I sat back down.

'Look, I do have a promotion available at the moment, and I really would like you to try out for the position. It was my daughter's job, you see.' He opened his wallet, showing me a photograph. Inside there was a woman with strawberry blonde hair and pale blue eyes. 'You remind me a little of her,' he said. 'And I don't mean the hair or the eyes – although yours are very similar. It's the forthrightness in your manner. And the way you strive to get to the truth of the matter at all times. I think you could do very well in this role.'

I pulled my eyes away from the picture. My hair hadn't got quite so much strawberry mixed in with the blonde, but I could see why he thought there were similarities. 'Why has your daughter left the job?' I wondered. 'Has she been promoted? Or moved to another of your papers?'

He shook his head. 'She's writing crime novels now,' he said. 'And she's loving every minute of it. She's tried to juggle the Daily Riddler and her own writing career, but it's no longer feasible.' He closed his wallet and put it in his breast pocket. 'I need to be upfront, though, Miss Smith. Other journalists have tried out for the position, and none have been successful. The Daily Riddler isn't your everyday paper. We need a certain sort of person there. I'm hoping you'll be that person, but I've hoped the same before. So there'll be a trial period involved. One week is the amount of time I've allotted for this. All of your travel expenses will be paid, along with your room and board.' He took a spoonful of his mud pie, a smile of satisfaction on his face as he tasted the dessert. 'So you see,' he said once he'd swallowed. 'This is not an act of charity on my part. Not at all. If it doesn't work out, you'll go back to the Daily Dubliner.'

I tried to eat some of my own dessert, but the coffee had made me sick to my stomach. Instead I moved it around the bowl, digesting everything he'd said. 'I've never heard of the Daily Riddler. And you mentioned travel and room and board. Where exactly is this job based?'

He stopped eating and looked hopefully my way. 'Are you saying you'll take part in the trial?'

'Maybe,' I replied with a shrug. 'Even though you *have* just made it sound like doctors in white coats are about to experiment on me. But … where *is* this job? And could I see a copy of the Daily Riddler?'

He pushed his empty bowl away and looked through his notebook once again. 'It's in Riddler's Edge,' he said. 'A lovely coastal town on the west of Ireland. You'll love it, I'm sure. And no, I don't have a copy of the Daily Riddler to hand at the moment, but you'll find it quite the interesting little paper. Or at least I hope so.' He pulled a page from his notebook and passed it my way. 'Everything you need to know is written down,' he said, opening his wallet again and throwing a wad of notes onto the table. 'Now, I've really got to be elsewhere. It was truly fascinating to meet you, Miss Smith. I hope to see you again.'

Before I could ask anything more, he picked up his cane and strode out of the café. I spun in my seat, looking out the window. But he sure moved fast for a guy with age-appropriate hips, because he was already gone.

3. Life Is But A Dream

The thing about growing up in the care system, is that you don't tend to accrue much stuff. Sure, you want stuff. You covet stuff. You might well drool at shelves full of books, wardrobes stuffed with clothes, and beds covered with cushions and cuddly toys galore. But you know that when the latest foster family have decided you're a bit strange, you won't get to take much more than one suitcase to the next family – who are also going to think you're a bit strange.

And old habits die hard, as the cliché goes. I'd gone through my adulthood in much the same way as my formative years. So when I arrived on the platform at Heuston Station the following Monday, I had one suitcase, a laptop bag, and a handbag. It was all that I'd need for a one-week stay, but it also happened to be everything I owned in the world.

I had checked and re-checked the timetable, oh, about a hundred times since Arnold Albright gave me my instructions. Much as I wished I was wrong, there was only one train going to Riddler's Edge that day, and it was leaving at five a.m. – so if I wanted to be on time for my meeting with the paper's editor, then getting up at crazy o'clock was a bit of a necessity.

The train was already there when I arrived. A stout man with a moustache and a whistle was marching up and down, saying, 'Last call for Riddler's Edge! Last call for the Riddler's Express!'

Last call? I glanced at my wristwatch, then at the clock on my phone just to be sure. It was ten minutes to five.

I looked at the train. It had a definite air of impatience about it, but I wish I could say that was the most remarkable quality. The train was old. Verging on antique. It sure wasn't expecting a lot of passengers, either. There were only two carriages.

'This is the train for Riddler's Edge?' I asked. 'It looks … well … it looks …' I paused, trying to think of a polite way to say that it looked like an exhibit from an old-timey museum. 'It looks … I mean, it's a long journey, isn't it? Is this train up to the job?'

The man looked me up and down and said, 'You getting on or what? Train's about to leave the station.'

I readjusted my stance, preparing to ask him why he was being so rude – I mean, it would have been fine for him to be ornery if I was actually late, but not when I was ten minutes early. He blew the whistle right in my face before I could work up a decent amount of bluster, then moved even closer to me and shouted, 'Doors are about to close on the Riddler's Express!'

I'm not usually one to stand down from an argument. Foster-mother number three, in fact, described me as a stubborn little goat. I found it a bit unfair at the time, I've got to say. I mean sure, a lot of kids *think* they want to run away with the circus. But I doubted a single one of those kids would have wanted to be in *her* circus. She was an elephant trainer. We disagreed about her methods, and I *might* have set some of the elephants free – and taken some footage of her training methods so that she'd never get to work with elephants again.

But I digress. Yeah, I was never one to stand down from an argument, and I *really* wanted to argue with this whistle-blower. And if the doors hadn't actually been closing, I might have told him precisely where he could stick his whistle. I settled for glowering in his general direction and picked up my suitcase, running onto the train. I was barely on board before the door shut behind me with a clang.

I looked around, feeling a tad wobbly after the exchange. I appeared to be in the train's dining car. A dining car that had a distinctly Poirot-esque quality. The tables were laid with white linen, and sparkling glasses and silverware were ready and waiting. For what, though? There was only one other woman in the carriage, and whilst I could imagine some passengers from the other carriage might fancy a snack sooner or later, did they really want silver service with their doughnuts and coffee?

I glanced at the other passenger. She was all wrapped up in black and wearing a pair of designer sunglasses. She waved over at me and patted the seat next to her. 'You must be the new reporter,' she said. 'Come and sit next to me.'

Seeing as the train had begun to lurch beneath me, I was going to need to sit somewhere, so it might as well be there. Although I couldn't see her face (her scarf and hat covered everything the sunglasses had left behind) her voice sounded old. I lugged my bags across and sat down. 'I'm Ash,' I said, extending a hand.

Her own gloved hands wrapped warmly around mine, and she said, 'I'm Bathsheba, my dear. It's *very* nice to meet you.'

She pulled a Thermos from her bag. 'Don't worry, I don't drink this early,' she said, laughing. 'It's just coffee. My husband makes me three flasks every time I have to go to Dublin for my medical treatment. One for the journey there, one to have in the hospital, and one for the journey back. He'd much rather come along with me, but I won't let him. He knows how much I hate my condition, and that I'd rather go through the treatment on my own, so he does the only nice thing that I'll let him do. He gives me a lovely kiss, then sends me on my way with the best coffee in the world. I'd offer you some, but I take quite a lot of sugar.'

'That's okay,' I said as I watched her slowly sip the drink. I wasn't about to ask her what she was doing in hospital, or the fact that I couldn't see even an inch of her skin, so I decided to ask her something less personal instead. 'It must be a very fancy Thermos,' I said. 'How long does it keep drinks warm?'

'Oh, at least two days,' she replied. 'Now, don't go getting disappointed when you get off the train. Riddler's Edge isn't a big town, but it's a good place to live. I don't actually live there myself – my house is in another town close by. But I'm staying there at the moment, and it really isn't as boring as it looks, so give it a chance. I'd love to see you stay longer than the last three journalists Arnold hired.'

I bit my lip. So she knew Arnold? I'd better tread carefully, then. 'Um, yeah. He mentioned he'd trialled a few people for the position before me. I guess his daughter's shoes are kind of big to fill.'

'Big?' She shook her head. 'Try enormous. But you have a nice look about you. I think you'll fit right in.'

I was just about to reply when the most surly-looking guy I'd ever seen arrived at the table. He was about eighteen or nineteen, with pale skin and red-rimmed eyes, and an expression that said he'd rather be anywhere but here. He was wearing a short-sleeved shirt that seemed to be made entirely of stains, and he had a silk scarf wrapped around his neck. 'I suppose you'll be needing a red smoothie soon,' he said to Bathsheba.

I heard the old woman gulp, and her voice was shaky when she spoke. 'Yes, Gunnar. That would be lovely.'

He grunted, jotted her order down and turned to me. 'What'll you have?'

'Is there a menu?' I asked.

As the train jerked on the tracks, his silk scarf slipped from his neck. He tied it in place almost immediately, but not before I'd managed to see an enormous tattoo, wrapping its way all around his neck. 'Vlad's Boys?' I read. 'Is that a band?'

He smirked and looked at Bathsheba. 'Ask the old lady. She knows *all* about Vlad's Boys.' He reached across to another table and threw a menu at me. 'Now, either order something or go into the next carriage, because these seats fill up fast.'

'Wow,' I said. 'Whoever does the hiring for the rail service should be taken out and shot. I'll have a red smoothie, too.'

He snorted. 'You don't want one of those.'

'He's right,' Bathsheba whispered. 'It's got an awful lot of iron in it. For senior citizens, only. It'll give you a tummy ache, dear.'

'Oh.' I looked over the menu. I wasn't used to eating this early, and would probably only get a coffee, but I was curious to see what was on offer. And maybe a very small part of me wanted to make him wait, too. The menu seemed to be divided into three sections. The first was titled: *Standard.* The second was titled: *Special Diets.* The third was titled: *Vegan.*

The standard menu was fairly, well, standard. I could get a toasted cheese sandwich, a croissant, some porridge or a full Irish breakfast. I flicked through to the vegan menu. There was a toasted vegan-cheese sandwich, a vegan croissant, porridge with a choice of soy, almond or oat milk, or a vegan Irish breakfast.

The special diets menu only had two items. There was the red smoothie, or something called a *Special Irish Breakfast.* According to the menu, it was served extra rare.

I closed the menu and handed it back to him. 'I'll just have a coffee.'

Gunnar grunted, then walked off into the kitchen area.

As he walked away, Bathsheba turned to me. 'He's a troubled young man. You'll find out all about him and his ilk if you decide to stay in town.'

I was going to ask her more when he returned with our drinks. Bathsheba's smoothie looked like it was bursting with berries, but she was probably right about the iron. It had a metallic smell that turned my stomach. Perhaps it was turning her stomach, too, because she had yet to touch a drop.

'Not to your taste?' I asked.

'Oh, I'll have it in a minute,' she said. 'I don't like to eat when it's dark.'

Seeing as I was still half-asleep, I went ahead and downed my coffee. I'd just finished when the door to the next carriage opened, and a couple of dozen people milled through. 'I'll move next door for a while,' I said. 'So someone else can have my seat.'

I couldn't be sure but I think she smiled, somewhere beneath the scarf, hat and glasses. 'You go on, my dear. Enjoy the journey.'

I brought my belongings into the next carriage. There was a shelving area close to the door, and I stowed my suitcase there while I looked around. There were plenty of seats empty, but I couldn't be sure if they were only temporarily vacated, while their occupiers were grabbing breakfast.

In one of the empty seats, about half way down the aisle, a guy gave me a grin that made my knees turn to jelly. He sat with his legs wide apart, patted the seat next to him and said, 'You can sit next to me. I promise I won't bite, darlin' – unless you want me to.'

Oh dear. I *really* hoped there were other options. Yes, I found him devastatingly attractive, but I wasn't altogether sure why. He was attractive in a way that had never turned me on before. He was long-haired and skinny, which just didn't do it for me. He looked like he loved himself, too, which *definitely* didn't do it for me. And also – just a minor point – there was a woman sitting across from him who glared at him and hissed, 'What are you *doing,* Jasper? You said *I* was your forever girlfriend!'

I was just about to go and hide in the loo, when a female voice called out, 'You can sit here!'

I looked in the direction of the voice. A tall woman was standing up at the back of the train. She had braided, dark hair, and she appeared to be wearing … I squinted, wondering if all of those eye tests had been wrong after all. The woman definitely seemed to be wearing what I thought she was – some sort of jumpsuit, with a silver breastplate on top.

But hey, what did I know? I was a twenty-nine year old who wore flat boots every day, *and* I'd worn the same style of jeans since I was fifteen. I hadn't left my fashion sense behind – I'd never had one in the first place. Silver breastplates could be the latest thing.

I shuffled along the centre aisle, glancing through the windows as I walked. It was still dark outside, and there were plumes of smoke, rising all around the exterior of the train. Maybe this thing really was as old as it looked. I could just picture the engine room right now – some poor guy shovelling coal like crazy, wearing a flat cap and a red neckerchief.

When I reached the seat I sank into it, smiling gratefully at the woman. 'Thanks so much,' I said. 'This train is a *lot* busier than I thought it would be, considering it's going to a town I only heard of last Friday.'

She smiled at me. 'I know. I keep saying they need an extra carriage, but no one ever listens to me. I'm Gretel, by the way.' She extended a hand.

'I'm Ash,' I said, shaking her hand and glancing at the two seats opposite.

Each seating area in the carriage was arranged like a booth, with two long seats facing one another and a table in between. There were two guys across from us. One was a teenager, with short blond hair. He was slurping a carton of chocolate soymilk and reading a comic. He gave me a brief wave, then returned his attention to his comic.

The other guy … well, I had no idea what he looked like, because he was wearing the exact same get-up as Bathsheba had been. Sure, his glasses were a different style, and his scarf, hat and gloves were woollen, but just as with Bathsheba, I couldn't see an inch of his skin.

I looked at the woman again. She wasn't just tall. She was practically Amazonian. She seemed to be leafing casually through a magazine, but there was something alert about her. Every few seconds, I could have sworn I saw her eyes dart to the window.

I pulled my e-reader from my bag and turned it on. I had some good books on there. Surely one of them would be exciting enough to take my mind off the fact that this whole morning was a little bit odd. I opened up a fantasy novel I'd been reading, and tried to concentrate on the words. But all the while, the events of the last few days were going through my mind. My special notebook. My lunch with Arnold. And now this train.

I'd long grown used to odd. My life had been filled with it, after all. But usually I had people telling me that *I* was the strange one, that I was seeing weirdness where it simply didn't exist. Since my meeting with Arnold, though, I'd started to wonder.

I had done an internet search on the Daily Riddler. There wasn't a single mention of it online. I did find the town of Riddler's Edge, though. Apparently it had a population of two hundred and three. And yet there was a busy train making its way there, each and every day.

When I was a kid and I was trying *not* to notice odd things happening around me, I used to play an old song over and over in my head. You probably know the one: *Row, Row Row Your Boat.*

So I sang it now, inside my mind, hoping it would calm me down the same way it had back then. I'd gotten as far as the *Merrily, merrily, merrily, merrily* line, when the covered-up man opposite me began to sing in his sleep. His voice was low and even as he sang, '*Life is but a dream.*'

My eyes darted towards him. Judging by the way he was sitting, slumped in the seat, it was fairly safe to assume he was sleeping. But was he? I glanced at Gretel.

'You okay?' she asked.

I bit my lip. 'This might sound strange,' I whispered, shuffling closer to her. 'But … did I just sing out loud?'

Her brow furrowed. 'No.' She nodded at the covered-up man. '*He* just sang out loud. He does that sometimes, in his sleep.'

'In his sleep? Are you a couple?'

A burst of laughter escaped her. 'Me? And Dylan Quinn? As if! No, I've just been on the train with him before, that's all.' She glanced out the window. Daylight was beginning to creep its way through the clouds. Her alert expression increased, and she gave me a tight smile and turned back to her magazine.

I looked back down at my e-reader, trying to find some other way to calm down. I mean, so what if that man in black just happened to finish off a song that I was only singing in my mind? It was probably just a weird coincidence. Right?

The train stopped a few times; no one got off but three more people got on. As the morning wore on and the light grew stronger, Gretel suddenly sat up and tapped the man she'd called Dylan on the arm.

'Wake up, dummy,' she said. 'It's light out.'

He jerked in his seat, then sat up. After a moment or two, he pulled off his glasses, his hat, his scarf and his gloves. And while he took it all off, I … well, I stared.

I mentioned that my attraction to that long-haired guy in the carriage was bizarre, considering he was *not* my type – and clearly a creep. But this man … I gulped. This man was *definitely* my type. As he pulled off his hooded sweater, I could see just how closely the T-shirt he wore beneath was moulded to his torso. His hair was as black as coal, and his eyes were very nearly black, too. His lips were so deeply coloured that I wondered if he was wearing make-up.

He wiped his eyes, looked my way, and gave me a little grunt that I guess *could* have been a greeting. Then he folded his arms and slumped back down.

'Do *not* go back to sleep, Dylan,' Gretel said, tapping him on the arm again.

'Oh, for the goddess's sake!' he exclaimed. 'Why shouldn't I go back to sleep? I'm tired after all that prodding and poking at the hospital.'

Gretel's eyes narrowed, and she nudged her head in my direction while she stared at Dylan. 'This is the new reporter,' she said, emphasising every single word. 'You know – Arnold's latest.'

Dylan's eyes shot open and he looked me up and down. I watched a vein pulse in his neck, and a hungry look entered his eyes. Oh my.

'Hi. It's em … it's nice to meet you,' he said, licking his lips.

'And *this*,' said Gretel to me, 'is Detective Dylan Quinn. He works out of Riddler's Edge garda station. And right now, he's about to head off to the dining car and grab himself a nice smoothie. Aren't you, Dylan?'

His eyes didn't leave my face, but he stood up and shuffled out past the comic-reading kid. 'Yeah,' he said. 'Yeah, I think I really need my smoothie.'

As soon as he was gone, Gretel's whole demeanour relaxed. 'Sorry about him,' she said. 'He's not too keen on having to get the early morning train.' She seemed about to say more, when we heard the detective's voice booming from the dining car.

'Hurry it up, will you Gunnar?' he was barking.

Gretel stood up. 'Actually, you know what? I think I'll just go and get myself something, too.'

As I watched her walk away, I noticed that she had a truncheon hanging off her belt. I peered more closely. It was definitely a truncheon. Maybe she was a garda, too. The train lurched, and she tripped over. Over *what*, I wasn't sure. It seemed like she'd fallen over her own feet.

As she'd fallen, though, the truncheon had flown off her belt. It bounced along the floor of the carriage, and landed at my feet. I picked it up and was about to bring it over to her, when I noticed it wasn't as similar to a garda truncheon as I'd first thought. It had more of a taper to it. My hand tingled, and the truncheon began to waver in front of my eyes. I closed my lids, and opened them again. The truncheon wasn't wavering, not exactly. It was just doing that thing that objects seemed to do when I suffered one of my migraines – it was as if I was looking at it through a kaleidoscope.

'Ash?' Gretel was standing beside me, reaching out for her truncheon. 'Are you all right?'

I handed it back to her. 'Yeah. Yeah, sorry. Just spaced out for a second. Don't mind me.'

She looked at me for a moment more, but the detective's voice bellowed out of the dining car again, so she turned tail and ran.

I was just about to sit back and pretend to read my book again, when I heard a blood-curdling scream, followed by someone crying out, 'She's dead! Someone's poisoned Bathsheba Brookes!'

4. There Has Most Definitely *Not* Been a Murder on the Riddler's Express

I sat up, staring in the direction of the scream. The Amazonian woman was barging through the door into the dining carriage, so I did what any nosey reporter would – I leapt out of my seat and followed.

The dining carriage was deathly quiet, while people stared down at Bathsheba's body. Dylan Quinn and Gretel were closest, and they both seemed to be examining the body whilst the others kept a respectful distance. It made sense for Dylan to be there, seeing as Gretel had told me he was a detective. But what about Gretel? I was sure her truncheon wasn't garda issue.

I edged my way closer. The old lady's body was covered with a rash, and boils were everywhere. She looked like she'd been exposed to something toxic. She'd removed her sunglasses and gloves at some point, and done so willingly, because they were sitting neatly on top of the table where she and I had been sitting.

'Has back-up been called?' I asked, sinking to my knees to take a closer look. I'd seen plenty of poisonings during my time at the Daily Dubliner, but none where the body looked like *this*. But the person who shouted out that Bathsheba had been poisoned sounded certain of the fact. 'Her coffee flask will need to be tested,' I said. 'And she had something called a red smoothie to drink, so that'll need to be looked into, too.'

Gretel looked at Dylan, her perfect brows lifted in question. He let out a low growl of irritation. 'Deal with her,' he said to Gretel.

Gretel stood up and dropped something she was holding – a long, black gadget with a green flashing light. As she stooped to pick it up, the detective gave her a tense smile and handed it to her.

Gretel took it quickly, then shoved it into a pocket and out of sight. Seeing as she had been happily brandishing it a moment ago, it seemed like she was hiding it from *me* rather than the others in the carriage. But why?

She cleared her throat and looked pointedly at me. 'Civilians need to keep away from the body,' she said. 'Nothing personal, Ash. You should go back to your seat. We'll be pulling into the station in a few minutes.'

I looked around the carriage. 'Why should I go back to my seat? Nobody else is.'

'They are.' Gretel pushed open the door into the adjoining carriage. 'See.' She nodded towards an old woman, sitting in a seat at the centre of the carriage, happily knitting away as though nothing was happening. 'Hi Norma! Lovely morning, isn't it?' Gretel gave the woman a wave.

Norma looked up from her knitting. 'Beautiful. Another dead one, dearie?'

Gretel shrugged her shoulders. 'Probably just an allergic reaction, same as last time.'

Norma nodded, seeming entirely satisfied with that explanation. 'Isn't it always?' she said, and turned her attention back to the green scarf she was crafting.

I eyed Gretel warily. 'What are you? An undercover garda or something?'

'Or something,' she said. 'Just sit down and enjoy the rest of the journey. Detective Quinn has everything in hand.'

I stood on my tiptoes, peering over her shoulder. The detective looked so different than when he first awoke. Now, he was alert and organised. He held a notebook open in his hands, and was questioning the people in the dining carriage. But wait one cotton picking minute! There was a newcomer in there, a stout man on his knees beside Bathsheba's body. He must be a doctor, I supposed. And he wasn't the only sudden arrival. There were three other newcomers, all wearing the same strange get-up as Gretel.

I was just about to ask what the hell was going on, when the train lurched to a stop, knocking me against the door, the back of my head hitting it with a thud as I fell. But I wasn't about to let a case of possible concussion stop me. I stood up, rubbing my head and pointing into the dining carriage. 'When did they get on?' I asked. '*How* did they get on?'

Gretel gave me an innocent shrug. 'Just now, of course. The second the train stopped. And seeing as we've pulled into the station, you're probably okay to go.' She glanced back at Detective Quinn. 'She and Norma can head off now, can't they, Dylan?'

He glanced up at me, then looked away. 'Yeah, get them out of here. Everyone else stays on.'

I stood my ground. 'Look,' I said, ignoring the dizziness that had come on after the knock to the head. 'I spoke with Bathsheba when I first got on the train. Surely someone ought to interview me, at least.'

'All in good time.' Gretel forced a smile while she reached into the luggage area and pulled out my suitcase. 'They'll be expecting you at the Vander Inn.' She placed my case in my hands, and slung my laptop bag over my shoulder, while I stood there, mutely. ‘Well, have a lovely stay in Riddler’s Edge.’

5. The Vander Inn

I stood on the platform, watching Norma stride across a bridge that stretched above the tracks. She was wearing her work-in-progress, knitting the green scarf and using it to keep warm at the same time. She was humming happily as she knitted, as if gruesome death was an everyday occurrence here in Riddler's Edge. Although, given the conversation she'd had with Gretel, maybe it was. What was it Norma had said? 'Another dead one, dearie?'

The station itself was yet another oddity in an oddity-filled morning. It was just as ancient as the train, although not nearly as well-kept. There was an empty ticket booth, a toilet I wouldn't pee in if you paid me, and a bench outside covered by a rotten wooden awning. Even though the morning was dead still, every part of the building creaked.

I looked down at Arnold's instructions:

A room has been reserved for you at the Vander Inn, directly across from the train station at

Riddler's Edge. Cross the railway bridge and turn right. You can't miss it.

Gretel had mentioned the place I was to be staying. Even Bathsheba had known who I was when I boarded the train. No doubt the people at the Vander Inn would know my blood type, dress size and favourite colour.

I looked across the bridge. Norma was off in the distance now, turning to the left, towards a modern-looking building. From the back, it looked like a convenience store. There were a few other buildings along the same road, and they were an odd mixture of modern and ancient. Was it too much to hope that the Vander Inn would be one of the newer places?

I sighed. Yeah, yeah it was definitely too much to hope for. Even though I still hadn't set foot on the bridge, I already knew which one the Vander Inn was. It was the one that looked Victorian, creepy, and – although I couldn't tell this simply from the back of the three storey house – it *kind* of looked like it might be lacking in indoor plumbing, too.

As I neared the opposite side of the bridge, I spied the sign swaying in the stillness – *The Vander Inn. Hot and cold running water available.* I gulped. Hot and cold running water should not be something you needed to advertise on a sign. It should be a given.

I hovered on the spot, wondering if now would be a good time to just turn tail and run. Maybe that was what my predecessors had done. Maybe they hadn't even made it past day one of the week-long trial.

But whatever about the other reporters, none of this should be fazing me the way it was. I mean, I was a girl who had lived with over a dozen foster families. And the elephant trainer wasn't even the worst of the bunch.

There had been the family of stunt people who sent me back to the orphanage when I baulked at jumping a horse through a flaming hoop. There had been the family of bankers who washed their hands of me when I spent my pocket money on sweets and magazines instead of depositing it in a high-interest savings account. There was the foster-father who couldn't understand why I didn't declare him the One True God the way his other children did, or the amateur astronomer foster-mam who believed her alien lover had given her the blueprints for three of her telescopes. Actually, I'd liked her, and she seemed to like me too. I'd only returned to the orphanage because she disappeared in a blinding flash of light one night.

Hmm, maybe I should wait a while before I reveal information like that. I realise that, when I list these things out, one after the other, the events of my life can sound a little on the farcical side. But that kind of life can have its upsides. Like today, for instance. Sure, I wanted to run back to my tiny, unhomely flat. And yeah, my job in the Daily Dubliner's basement was suddenly looking like a wonderful position. But I'd been through worse than this.

I squared my shoulders, sang *Row, Row, Row Your Boat* inside my mind (my voice was far less screechy that way) and walked towards my lodging house.

When I pushed the gate open, it let out a high-pitched squeal that I'm sure people could hear all the way back in Dublin. There was an ornate porch above an elegant red door, and one of those bells you pull was hanging next to the door. Like the door itself, the bell was in surprisingly good nick. In fact, now that I was no longer looking at the house from a fearful distance, the whole place appeared a great deal nicer than I'd expected. There were daffodils and ferns in little pots, and a doormat with the word *Welcome* spelled out in pretty scrolled writing.

I reached for the doorbell, and tugged.

Oh dear. Forget what I said about this place being nicer closer up. It wasn't nicer. In fact, it was about a hundred times scarier. Because the tune that the doorbell played was *Row, Row, Row Your Boat*.

A moment after the disturbing ditty finished, the door was pulled open by a woman who looked close to my age. She was wearing jeans and a gypsy shirt, and had silver jewellery draping off just about every body part it could. She wore vivid make-up, and had long black hair, reaching almost to her waist.

She squinted a little, then stood back in the shadows. 'You must be Aisling Smith,' she said, extending a hand laden with more rings than she had fingers. One of them stood out in particular. The stone was an odd shade of green, a shade that made me feel a little dizzy. 'I'm Pru. Come on in.'

I followed Pru into a wide, stunning hallway. The tiles on the floor were black and white, and the walls were painted a calm shade of cream. There were portraits and ornaments everywhere, but the hall was so large that it didn't seem claustrophobic.

'My mother runs the establishment,' she told me. 'But I help out now and then, when I'm not too busy with my fortune-telling work. Would you like some breakfast, or would you rather see your room first of all?'

My stomach began to growl. It was almost nine, and usually I'd have wolfed down some porridge at six-thirty and be searching for a snack right about now. 'Breakfast would be wonderful,' I said.

She smiled. 'Just leave your bags there. The housegh– the em, the house*boy* will bring them up to your room.'

She led the way into a dining room that reminded me of the dining car on the train –

tablecloths, vases, the whole shebang. The smell coming from the kitchen was divine, and there was one resident finishing off his meal.

His skin was paper-thin, but despite his age he kept himself looking well. His suit was neatly pressed and elegant, and his shoes were gleaming. He was eating a plate of what looked like black pudding, and sipping at a coffee. As soon as I entered the room, he placed his knife and fork neatly on his plate and turned.

'You've been on the train,' he said, gazing at me with watery eyes. 'Somebody died.'

I blinked. 'I … how did you know that?'

Pru patted his arm. 'Hush now, Donald. Let her settle in.'

'But you can smell it just as well as I can, Pru. And Bathsheba should have been *here* by now.'

While I stared down at the doily-strewn tablecloth, wondering how the hell to field *that* one, Pru gave him a sympathetic look, patting his arm again. 'Go on now, Donald. Go on and go up to bed for the day, and I'll let you know as *soon* as Bathsheba returns.'

As the old man walked away, Pru sat down across from me. 'She died, didn't she? Bathsheba died on that train.'

I swallowed. 'I … yes. A woman called Bathsheba died in the dining car. How did you know?'

She sat back and folded her arms. 'My bedroom looks out onto the platform. I saw you and Norma get off, and no one else. They only keep people on the train when there's been a murder.'

I was trying to decide how to digest that when another woman walked in. She didn't look much older than Pru, but Pru looked up at her and said, 'Hello, Mam. This is Aisling Smith. Aisling, this is my mother, Nollaig.'

Her mother gave me a warm smile. 'Of course, of course. Now, I wasn't told if you have any dietary preferences.' She gave me an odd sniff. 'Oh, you'll probably just want the usual sort of breakfast, then. Sausages and eggs and the like?'

'That'd be great,' I said, my stomach letting out another rumble.

She and Pru rushed off to the kitchen. There was only a door separating it from the dining room, and I could hear them whispering back and forth. Arnold's name was mentioned a lot. Mine was mentioned almost as much. But what was said *about* Arnold and me, I couldn't quite work out. After a couple of minutes they walked back in, Nollaig carrying a plate piled high with food, while Pru carried a pot of coffee and some toast.

'Did you both know Bathsheba, then?'

Nollaig sat down and sighed. As soon as she was sitting across from me, I noticed she was wearing the same green-stoned ring as her daughter.

'Bathsheba has been with us a few weeks. She's been having treatment in Dublin, and it helps her to be close to the station. She and Donald have a home in another town nearby.'

I looked down at my food, wanting to eat but also feeling so sorry for him. Pretty soon, someone would be giving him the bad news. I hoped for his sake that it wasn't Detective Quinn. The man didn't seem like the sympathetic sort.

'I know how you feel, love,' said Nollaig. 'But you starving yourself silly isn't going to make Donald feel any better, now is it?'

I looked up at her, laughing weakly. 'What are you? A mind-reader?'

Nollaig and Pru shared a glance. Then Nollaig rose, patted me on the shoulder and said, 'Eat up, love. You'll need all the energy you can muster, if you're going to be able to deal with us lot.'

She sauntered off to the kitchen, curvaceous hips swaying behind her, and Pru sprang up and said, 'I'll go and make sure your room is ship-shape. It's on the top floor – room number nine. You've got your own bathroom, and there's a phone if you need to ring down for anything.'

≈

After breakfast I was stuffed to the gills and exhausted. Both Pru and her mother had disappeared, and the whole house had a sleepy silence about it that made me want to curl up beneath the covers. But I only had an hour to get ready for my meeting with the editor at the Daily Riddler, so I rushed to my room to prepare.

There was a wooden plaque on the wall beside the staircase, listing the room numbers and the floors they could be found on. My room, number nine, seemed to have the top floor all to itself. I wasn't sure if that meant I was getting a nice penthouse suite, or if I was being segregated in a cobwebby attic. But if the previous reporters had been anything to go by, I was unlikely to be here very long, so it probably shouldn't matter how cobwebby my room was. It wasn't as though I had a deathly fear of spiders or anything. I was only afraid of the ones that had eight legs.

As I sped up the stairs, I got the distinct impression that something cold and filmy rushed right past me. What was it Pru had seemed about to say before she revised her words to *houseboy*? Could she actually have been about to tell me a houseghost was bringing my bags upstairs?

I shook my head, refusing to look back at the cold, filmy form, and continuing on up to the third floor. There was a small landing up there, and only one door. It clearly stated that it was number nine, so I pushed it open.

As the room was revealed, I stood on the threshold, gasping. The room was … well … the room was amazing. Sure, it was just as old-fashioned as the rest of the house. But I was beginning to realise that sometimes, old-fashioned was good. I mean, I had a four-poster bed for criminy's sake. Through the open bathroom door I could see a huge, claw-foot bath, and the toilet had one of those overhead cisterns with a pull-chain.

There were French doors draped in gauzy white curtains, which seemed to lead out onto a balcony. In front of the doors there was an antique telescope. I examined it for a few seconds, a broad smile making its way across my face. My favourite foster-mother had a few like this in her collection, and my mind was suddenly thrust back to the nights we spent staring at the stars together.

As I cautiously opened the French doors, I realised that my room didn't just have a balcony. It wrapped around the entire third storey, and even had steps leading up to a widow's walk on the roof, giving me a view of the entire town. The surface looked stable, so I took a step out and walked around.

Arnold had told me this place was a coastal town, but he hadn't explained the smell, the view, the gorgeous white sand, the lovely little harbour with the fishing boats and what looked like an olde-worlde tavern a little to the north.

I rolled the telescope towards the doors and took a look through the lens. I focused on the tavern first, on the people walking in and out. There was a man with a pipe in his mouth, making me wonder, once again, if I'd entered some sort of time warp. A sign hung off the front of the place – *the Fisherman's Friend.* I spun the telescope to the right, and saw a lighthouse a short distance from the harbour. I heard my breath intake, just a little. Lighthouses and me … well, let's just say I find them sexy and leave it at that.

Okay, let's not leave it at that. I mean, I've already spilled way too much embarrassing information, so what difference will a little more make? I don't just find lighthouses sexy. I dream about them. I fantasise about them. I have invented a hundred scenarios in my mind, of living in a lighthouse with a sexy, barefooted man who makes amazing coffee and likes to do carpentry in his spare time.

He also enjoys midnight swims, impromptu picnics, and listening to David Bowie. He has a telescope set up on the top floor of his lighthouse, and he knows almost as much about the stars as Janette (my favourite foster mother). Oh, and because I don't have *remotely* high expectations, he happens to be an amazing lover, too.

I spun the telescope a little further to the north, and stood back, wiped my eyes and looked again. A sudden haze had fallen, although the sky looked clear just about everywhere else. That haze …

I went back inside and sat on my amazing bed, deep in thought. That haze had the same shimmering quality as the haze I'd seen between

Let's Go Round the Bend and *Times of Yore*. For the first time in my life, I felt absolutely certain that this was *not* a migraine.

A sense was beginning to fill me, but it wasn't a sense of foreboding. I felt like I was opening. Like I was about to embark on the most exciting experience of my life. This town was the strangest place I'd ever seen – and I'd seen a whole lot of strange. But despite it all, I felt completely at home.

6. The Daily Riddler

When I was a kid, I always had this notion that reporters should look a certain way – a snazzy suit, maybe a pair of glasses. But I was cursed with perfect eyesight (other than the aforementioned hazy moments), and I had yet to find a snazzy suit that I felt comfortable wearing. I'd bought one after my lunch with Arnold, along with some very grown-up shoes, hoping to make a good impression on the paper's editor.

But the fancy new outfit was still sitting on my four–poster bed, while I was in a sweater dress, knee-high flat-soled boots, and a faux-leather jacket. No matter how snazzy I *wanted* to look, I knew my limitations. I'd wind up tripping over my own feet if I wore my new shoes, and as for the fitted skirt and jacket I'd purchased, well … it just hadn't felt like *me.*

When I came out through the Vander Inn's screechy front gate, I turned right as per Arnold's directions. The main street wasn't exactly a happening place. There was that little convenience store Norma had been heading to, off to the left of the Vander Inn. There were a few pretty cottages on either side of the main street. There was a school, a church, a small garda station, and then … well then there was the Daily Riddler.

It was a large office, arranged over two floors. It had stunning glass doors with huge, circular brass handles. I put on my confident face, and walked inside.

A few feet inside the office, there was a short, immaculately-groomed man standing behind a walnut reception desk, speaking into the phone. As soon as he saw me he beamed, then quickly finished his call and extended a hand.

'You must be Aisling,' he said. 'Welcome to the Daily Riddler. I'm Malachy – receptionist by day, chef by night.'

'Chef?' I smiled at him. 'At the Fisherman's Friend? Or is there somewhere else in town?'

He began to readjust a perfectly neat pile of papers on the desk. 'I've just opened a little place. It's out the road a bit,' he replied vaguely. 'Quite out of the way. Anyway, why don't I bring you up to Grace now?'

I looked down at my notebook. Grace O'Malley was the editor here. I hadn't been able to find any previous publications she'd been in charge of when I looked her up online.

I followed Malachy up a sweeping, spiral staircase, and when we reached the top we came to a set of double doors, even more fabulous than the ones at the front of the building. Malachy pressed a brass buzzer, and a moment later a woman opened the doors.

She had long, golden hair, falling in fifties-style waves to her shoulders. Her lips were painted a deep red, and her outfit made me drool.

'Huh,' she said. 'So … you're Aisling Smith.'

I nibbled on my lower lip. 'No need to sound so disappointed,' I said, hoping I came across as jokey rather than sarcastic. The truth was, I was struggling *not* to be snarky. Grace was regarding me like I was that last, unsolvable word in an already irritating crossword puzzle.

'Shall I get you two some refreshments?' Malachy asked.

'I'm fine for now,' I said. 'But thanks.'

'I'll have my usual,' said Grace, leading me inside to what seemed to be half office, half private apartment. 'That is if you're okay with *carrying* it up?'

Malachy nodded quickly. 'Of course. I'll carry it. But don't blame me if some of it gets spilled along the way.'

The place was just as glamorous as the rest of the office. There was a sunken seating area with shag carpeting, a huge desk with an old-school typewriter, and a set of open double doors which showed me her magnificent bedroom beyond.

'Wow, talk about glam,' I said. 'I love the décor.'

Grace smiled and took a seat behind her desk, indicating that I should sit facing her. As I sat into the chair, she picked up a gold-handled magnifying glass, and looked through it at me. 'Huh,' she said, placing it down. 'So what do you think to the town, Aisling?'

'Call me Ash,' I said. 'And as for the town … well, mismatched is a word that comes to mind.'

She let out a peal of laughter. 'Yes. We all seem to be stuck in our own definitive time zones here. But it's not all like that. You'll find most of the town is perfectly … normal. Now, I've been informed of the incident on the train. I've already written up a piece.' She rummaged through a pile on her desk and pulled a page out, passing it to me. 'This is for tomorrow's daily edition. The piece for the evening paper isn't yet prepared. Tell me what you think.'

Well, what I *thought* was: what the heck could a town with a population of two hundred and three need with two editions per year, let alone per day? But I pasted a business-like smile on my face, and scanned the short article.

Unfortunate Death on the Riddler's Express

Yesterday morning, on the early morning train from Dublin to Riddler's Edge, an unfortunate incident occurred. Bathsheba Brookes, 85, died from an allergic reaction after consuming a meal containing nuts.

Relatives have been informed.

I read it over again, then again. During my fourth reading, Malachy appeared, placing a cup of black coffee on Grace's desk and then scurrying back down below.

'Problem?' Grace enquired, taking a sip from her cup.

'I … no. Well, yes, actually. Did you speak with the coroner's office? Did they confirm it was an allergic reaction *already*? I mean, Bathsheba and another guy on that train were totally covered up and wearing sunglasses while it was still dark, and there's no *way* it was a fashion statement. And also, what about this treatment Bathsheba was getting up in Dublin? Shouldn't we be looking into what medical conditions she might have had? Shouldn't the *coroner*? Who, by the by, arrived *far* too fast for my liking. This is the back of beyond, and yet the emergency services arrive on the scene faster than they do at a gangland murder in Dublin? And what's with having *two* editions? Per day? I just …'

I paused to take a breath, and also to wonder: why was she smiling? She should be scowling, surely, after a tirade like that.

She picked up the magnifying glass and looked at me once more. 'Hmm,' she said. Then she added a, 'Huh,' just for good measure. She lowered the magnifying glass and said, 'People have quite the appetite for puzzles in this town. They buy both editions so they can do extra crosswords and the like. *That's* why we have two editions per day.'

'Right.' I crossed my arms. 'Arnold didn't have a copy of the paper to hand when we spoke last Friday. I don't suppose you could show me one right now? I'd *love* to see a copy of the evening edition.'

She cleared her throat and looked off into the distance. 'You know, we're really into recycling here at the Daily Riddler. This evening's edition is off at the printers. I'll try to keep a copy back for you, but I can be quite forgetful.'

'Well, I'll be able to pick it up in the local shop, surely?'

She was still staring off into that fascinating spot somewhere in the distance. 'Oh, we do a very small run of the evening edition. I doubt you'll find a copy.'

I sat back and stared at her. 'Huh.'

'Indeed,' she said. 'Now, I'm pairing you up with Greg, our IT guy and photographer, for your trial. Tell him to take some photos and do his thing.'

I could feel my eyes begin to bulge. She was actually giving me a story? 'Photos of what, exactly? What are we working on?'

She finally met my eyes. 'The train will be doing a run to Dublin in an hour's time. Get over to the station before it leaves, nose around. See if you can come up with anything more … interesting … than the allergy angle. Oh, and go and talk to the husband afterwards. It's always good to get a … human … angle on these things. Bathsheba lived a long and interesting life. People will enjoy reading about it.'

I was about to ask, oh, I don't know, maybe a hundred more questions, when she stood up and pressed a button on her desk. The doors opened behind me, and she turned away, sauntered into her bedroom, and slammed the door.

≈

Malachy told me that I would find Greg in the break room, so I made my way there. It was just as elegant as the rest of the place, with curved couches, an expensive-looking coffee machine and shelves filled with books.

There was only one person in there. He had tight-cut blond hair, pale blue eyes, and was tall and wiry looking. He had a laptop open in front of him, and was wearing headphones with a mouthpiece. He was speaking quickly, typing and hitting his mouse like his life depended on it, frantically chewing a chocolate bar and slurping coffee at the same time.

‘Greg?’ I asked.

He jumped, said, ‘Got to go,’ into his mouthpiece, and then stared at me. ‘Sorry. I was in the middle of fighting the War of the Enclaves.’

I looked enviously at his empty coffee cup. Maybe that was what I needed. Another shot of caffeine. Or two. Perhaps then I’d catch up with whatever it was he’d just said. ‘The War of the Enclaves? That means nothing to me.’

‘It’s a game,’ he said, as though I ought to know. ‘Set in ancient times, back when the faeries and the witches were fighting for supremacy. I was playing the faerie side. Obviously.’

‘Obviously. So … I’m Ash. The latest reporter on trial here.’

‘Yeah.’ There was a tired tone to his voice. ‘I kind of figured that. Do you need me to set your computer up?’

‘No. Well, maybe later. Grace said we should go to the train station together? So you can take some photos. And then …’ I did my best to withhold a sigh. ‘And then we’re supposed to go speak with Bathsheba’s husband.’

‘Oh. Did she say I should do anything else, other than take photos?’

I shrugged. ‘She said, “Tell Greg to take some photos and do his thing.”’

‘Ah.’ His eyes lit up. ‘I’ll get my equipment.’

I followed him into a messy corner office, where he slung a camera around his neck. He picked up some other equipment too, but he turned his back to me while he did so, and by the time he'd turned back around I couldn't see what he'd packed into his bag. 'Come on then,' he said, bounding out of his office. 'No time like the present.'

He moved so fast, and had a proper bounce to each step. I was glad I'd chosen my comfy old boots instead of the high heels, but even with flat soles I barely managed to keep up with him. By the time I joined him on the street, I was panting.

'I have a van,' he said, pointing to a deep purple Volkswagen parked across the road. 'But the station's only a short walk. You up for a stroll?'

'Sure,' I said, catching sight of the ring on his finger. It looked exactly like the one Pru and her mother had been wearing. 'I really like that ring,' I told him. 'Pru – she lives at the Vander Inn – has the exact same one. Hey, do you two know each other?'

'Em … no?' he said, sounding unsure. 'Well, maybe a little bit. You … you're from Dublin, right? Anywhere I'd have heard of? Luna Park, maybe?'

I resisted the urge to gape at him. Luna Park was one of the place names on the list I'd been making in my special notebook.

'No,' I said, trying to sound casual. 'Not Luna Park.' I glanced at a strange-looking black gadget hanging off his belt. It looked exactly like the gadget Gretel had been waving about in the dining car. Greg hadn't been wearing it in the break room, though. Maybe he put it on when he turned his back to me at his desk. Much as I wanted to ask about it, I decided to hold back for now. People weren't answering any questions I asked today. Perhaps it was better to stop asking, and see what I could find out for myself.

≈

As we stood on the apex of the bridge, I could see that things were wrapping up on board the Riddler's Express. Staff members and passengers from the morning train were walking away, while those for the next journey were queuing at the doors, while a thin man in a garda uniform waved them slowly on.

I marched towards the garda.

'We're from the Daily Riddler,' I told him. 'Is it all right if we go in and take a few pictures?'

He shrugged. 'The body's gone, love, and dying from an allergic reaction to peanuts doesn't seem all that newsworthy to me. But if you fancy photographing a perfectly normal train, then be my guest.'

Just as the thin garda stood aside, I spotted Detective Quinn leaving the train. Beside him was the waiter who'd served Bathsheba and me earlier on in the dining carriage. The waiter was wearing cuffs, cuffs that had a kaleidoscope haze around them.

I stepped back from the door and walked towards Detective Quinn.

'You're making an arrest?'

He glowered at me. 'What's it to you?'

Yes, it was official – I hated this man. I hated him more than my third foster-father (a tuba player who insisted that I, too, become a tuba player and join the family's travelling band – it was the one time *I* asked to leave a family).

'What's it to me? I'm covering this story, Detective Quinn. And I find it a bit odd that you're arresting someone, considering Bathsheba's death was supposedly caused by an allergic reaction.'

He shoved the waiter into a nearby car and locked the door behind him. Then he turned back to me, his lips curled into the most irritating smile I'd ever seen.

'I don't like the way you said *supposedly* there, Lois Lane. It was an allergic reaction, plain and simple. No supposedly about it. And as for Mr Lucien over there.' He cast a sneer towards the car. 'I'm arresting him on a different matter. A matter that's none of your business.'

I took a step towards him. I was no Amazonian, sure, but he couldn't intimidate me with all of his handsome tallness. Wait – strike that from your memory. I'll rephrase my previous utterings to something more like … he couldn't intimidate me with his irritating everything.

'I'm a journalist, Detective Quinn. Which means I go out of my way to make *everything* my business. I want to know more about this arrest.' I pulled my notebook and pen from my front pocket. 'The young man's name is Gunnar Lucien, I know that much.'

He looked like he was chewing on his tongue, desperately trying to bite back some choice words. 'He's a thief, okay. It's a petty crime, not worth writing about.'

'Oh?' I kept my gaze steady on his. Which was kind of difficult, seeing as his dark eyes were blazing. 'What is he being accused of stealing? Do you intend to charge him or issue a warning? Does he have previous convictions? Have the stolen items been returned?'

A low growl came from the detective's throat. He turned to Greg, who had suddenly appeared beside me. 'Tell the new girl I'll submit my usual report to the newspaper when I'm good and ready.'

The detective climbed into his car, slammed the door, and took off out of the carpark.

For a moment I stood there, flabbergasted, staring after the car. It wasn't until I heard Greg clear his throat and say, 'I think we'd better get on with the photographs, maybe,' that I remembered I wasn't alone.

I kept my gaze on the car. A car that was now speeding *past* the garda station. 'Yeah, right. The photographs,' I said absentmindedly, running up onto the bridge, standing on the apex again where I'd get a better view. 'Oh, Greg,' I said sweetly. 'I don't suppose you'd happen to know why Detective Quinn is driving the suspect out of town?'

Greg stayed firmly planted on the platform. 'I imagine he has a perfectly good reason. A reason that he'll explain in his report to the newspaper later on. So why don't we just get on the train and get these photos taken?'

I grunted, still staring at the car. It had gone past the lighthouse now, and was speeding towards a hazy horizon. I narrowed my eyes. There it was, that area I'd spotted from my bedroom. It was *still* hazy, more than an hour later. The detective's car took a left turn and disappeared from my view.

'What's over that way?' I asked Greg, pointing to where I meant.

He shrugged his shoulders and walked back towards the train. 'Does it matter? Come on, Ash. We've got work to do.'

Feeling like I had a wasp hive in my stomach, I followed him into the dining car. The place had been cleaned up since I'd last been inside. There wasn't so much as a piece of crime-scene tape in sight. Greg began fiddling around with camera filters and taking photos.

'Why so many filters?' I asked as he stopped shooting and changed the filter yet again.

'I'm artsy,' he said.

Artsy my behind. But I'd already concluded that no one was going to answer my questions, so I left Greg to it and looked around the dining car. A young woman was placing fresh flowers in the vases. I cast a quick glance at Greg to make sure he was still busy being artsy, and sidled towards the girl.

'It's awful, isn't it?' I said in a low voice. 'About Bathsheba, I mean.'

She nodded, swallowing, pulling a strand of her dark brown hair out of her eyes. 'She was such a lovely woman. Always left me a big tip.'

I sighed sympathetically, patting her back, keeping a side-eye on Greg. He'd stopped taking photos and was now waving that long black gadget around. A green light was blinking on the gadget, and Greg seemed exceptionally excited by the fact.

'I just love people like Bathsheba,' I said to the waitress. 'I admire their bravery when faced with a condition like that. The way they can still manage to be decent, generous people, no matter what they're going through.'

'Exactly!' she said with a sniffle. 'Most people become so hopeless when they get the diagnosis, and I can't say I blame them. I mean, look at Detective Quinn. He used to be such a lovely man, back when he was just our plain old Dylan. But now … I mean, Gunnar *looks* shady I know, what with the Vlad's Boys tattoo and everything. But I hope he's not really like that. He couldn't be, could he? Not deep down. He's probably just easily led. He would never have killed–'

'Oh, there you are, Miriam!' Greg called out loudly, interrupting us. 'So sorry, I should have introduced you to Ash. Where are my manners? This is the new reporter on the Daily Riddler, Miriam. The *very* new reporter, working on the *daily* edition. The reporter who has just moved to town and has never lived anywhere like Riddler's Edge before.'

Miriam bit her bottom lip, her blue eyes widening.

'Forgive my colleague's rude interruption,' I said pleasantly. 'You were telling me you couldn't believe Gunnar would have killed Bathsheba?'

Miriam blinked, staring at Greg, opening and closing her mouth. 'I …' she said eventually. 'I …'

A crazy smile took over Greg's face. 'What? Killed? Wow, Ash, you must be in need of a bit of rest, what with getting the early morning train and all.'

I kept my expression even. 'Maybe.'

'Oh, hey, I bet you were wondering about this thing,' Greg said, pointing to the black gadget he'd been waving about a moment earlier. He had since placed it back on his belt-loop, and the green light was still blinking. 'Well, it's a pager,' he went on. 'I like old-school tech. I could probably get you one, if you wanted. Oh, and I could do some *amazing* stuff to your computer when I'm setting it up, too. Why don't we go back to the office and get started on that now?'

I narrowed my eyes. That thing was *not* a pager. No way, no how. Greg was trying to distract me, and he was doing a pretty bad job. 'Yeah, I'd love a pager,' I said. 'Y'know, for when I take my time travelling machine back to the nineties. Hey, why don't you just run off and call whoever was paging you, then? While I keep talking to Miriam here about why the detective thinks Gunnar killed Bathsheba.'

Greg swallowed, the crazed smile still on his face. 'Miriam *never* would have said Gunnar killed Bathsheba. Why would she? He stole some money from the cash register. How could he kill a woman who died from an allergic reaction to peanuts?' He rolled his eyes. 'The things you come out with. I can tell you're going to be an absolute hoot to work with.'

Miriam wore a smile mad enough to rival Greg's. 'Yeah, that's hilarious, Ash. I never said Gunnar was a killer. I said he was a *tiller*. It's … it's slang around here for people who steal from cash registers.'

'Right.' I nodded. 'That's what you said. Of course that's what you said.' I cast a tense smile at Greg and held up my notebook. 'I guess I'll have to correct these notes, then. It's a pity I never went modern, isn't it? I wouldn't have to make half as many corrections to my mistakes if I only used a recording device.'

'Yeah,' said Greg. 'But y'know – maybe the old ways are the best. You should definitely stick to the notebook.'

'Like you and your pager. You still haven't responded to the message you got there a minute ago. In fact, I think you must still be getting messages, because that green light is flashing a *lot.*'

He pulled his jacket across his so-called pager. 'Oh. Yeah. Yeah – that's just my mother. I'll call her as soon as I can. Listen, why don't we head on over to the Vander Inn? Get an interview with Bathsheba's husband. Grace said she wanted the human interest angle, right?'

I smiled sweetly. 'Sure, Greg. Whatever you say.'

7. Undying Love

When we arrived at the Vander Inn, Donald was sitting out on a stunning deck, watching the sea. He was wearing sunglasses, I noted. At least he was wearing them by day instead of by night. He was also wearing the same ring as Pru and Greg.

I pictured Bathsheba's body in my mind, and my heart began to drum. I'd been so focused on trying to figure out how she died that I hadn't taken it in at the time, but one of her gloveless fingers had *definitely* sported one of those green-stoned rings.

'Hello again, Donald,' I said softly. 'Do you remember meeting me this morning? I'm Aisling Smith, the new reporter from the Daily Riddler.'

He looked up at me, smiling sadly. 'Of course. It's the *daily* edition you're working on, isn't it?'

I kept my smile in place, nodding. There it was again – all the proof I needed that, should I ever get through this week-long trial, I'd be discovering a whole different newspaper.

'You'll have heard about my wife, I suppose,' Donald went on. 'You'll be wanting to ask me some questions too, I imagine. So the fine folks who live in Riddler's Edge can put their curious little minds at rest and stop wondering why there was such a hive of activity at the train station.'

I nodded again, sitting down across from him with my notebook in my hands. 'This is my least favourite part of being a reporter,' I admitted. 'It makes me feel like a vulture, preying on people's raw feelings, right after they've lost someone. All so I can write a few words in some paper that'll – most likely – be used to wrap up Christmas decorations or light the fire.'

He looked at me with interest. 'Funny, that's what I've always thought about newspapers myself.'

I laughed. 'That's what most people think, Donald. Especially when a loss is raw.'

'So then why *do* people talk to journalists?' he wondered.

I shrugged. 'Many reasons. If a death is suspicious, maybe they hope that reading about it in the newspaper will jog someone's memory.'

He looked away. 'Yes, but Bathsheba's death wasn't suspicious.'

'Of course not,' I replied quickly. 'But there are other reasons, too. It can help to talk about the person you've lost. Grace said that Bathsheba had lived a long and interesting life. Perhaps you could tell me some stories about her. We could do a piece on a life well lived, sort of thing.'

He looked at Greg, who was hovering a few feet behind me, fiddling with his filters again. ‘A life well-lived? Perhaps. I mean … I feel quite comfortable speaking to you, Miss Smith. I believe you’d do an admirable job telling Bathsheba’s story. But stories of a life like Bathsheba’s, well, they’re more *evening* material, don’t you think?’

Greg cleared his throat. ‘Probably. Listen, Ash, I’m not sure Grace had the right idea in sending us here. But maybe … maybe we should just leave Donald alone for now, yeah? If he wants to do some sort of memorial piece when he feels more up to it, he knows how to get in touch with us.’

I stood up without argument, hiding my confusion. I was positive that Donald would have given me an in-depth interview, had Greg agreed. So why *hadn’t* Greg agreed? Why was I sent here by Grace, only to be dragged off as soon as I was getting anywhere? Was this all part of the mysterious trial? Because if it was, I had no idea whether I was passing or failing.

Just as we were about to leave the deck, I turned back to Donald. ‘Y’know, there’s another reason why people talk to reporters. Same reason they can talk to therapists, or a stranger in the pub. Sometimes it’s easier, when you’re grieving, to talk to someone you don’t know.’ I squeezed his shoulder. ‘You know where I am, if you want an off-the-record chat.’

As I went to walk away, he called after me. 'Wait – Miss Smith. There is something I'd like you to write, about my Bathsheba.'

I turned back. 'Yes?'

'You can write … you can write that she always had my utmost, undying love.'

8. Norman Normal

I wandered around the shop, while Greg bought himself some lunch at the deli counter. For a convenience store in such a small town, it certainly had a lot of lunch-time customers. A lot of vegan food on the menu, too.

With my enormous breakfast still filling me up, I doubted I'd be hungry again until dinner time. As more people filed in, the shop began to get a little crowded, and I decided I'd be better off going outside to wait for Greg.

As I stepped outside I looked across the road, only to see yet another kaleidoscope-haze.

'It's weird, isn't it?' I turned to a grey-haired man sitting on a bench behind me. He was reading the Daily Riddler.

'What's weird, love?'

'The way the mist is settling in very specific areas only.'

He wrinkled his nose. 'What mist?'

'Across there.' I pointed.

'Don't see any mist there, love. I see a stretch of lovely green, with sheep grazing on it stretching all the way down to the beach. Maybe you need glasses?'

I felt my shoulders heave up and down. Yeah. Maybe the ten eye tests I'd had in the last five years had *all* been wrong. I had a good idea of how he was going to reply when I asked the question. But his answer had confirmed something. He didn't seem like he was lying. He seemed absolutely convinced that there was a green across the road, filled with happily-grazing sheep. I'd asked Greg about the haze as we walked into the shop, and his answer had been a jumpy, 'Huh? Yeah, yeah it's always a bit misty around here.'

So what did that mean? Some people in this town were clearly hiding things, but this man outside the shop, and the woman who'd been knitting on the train … those two didn't seem like they were hiding anything. They seemed completely oblivious.

'Are you local?' I asked.

'Lived here all my life, my darling,' he said. 'This is my shop.' He pointed to the sign above the door: *Norman's Shop.* 'I'm Norman. But you're definitely *not* local, are you love? That's a Dublin accent I detect.'

I sat down beside him. 'Yeah, I'm from the big smoke all right,' I said. 'Hey, Norman, are there some big businesses nearby or something? Or maybe some big housing development a little way out the road?'

He laughed as though I'd just told a joke. 'In Riddler's Edge? Would ya go on, would ya? Sure, what you see is what you get.'

I sincerely doubted that. I cast an eye back into the shop. 'So … where do all the customers come from, then? The queue is out the door.'

He followed my eyes, shrugging. 'I imagine they're just travelling through. We get a lot of people just passing through.'

'Huh.' I looked up and down the street. If all of these people were passing through, then why were the parking spaces in front of the shop empty? 'Is there a large carpark somewhere, then?'

Again, he laughed like I was a prize joker. 'For what? Sure there's hardly anyone in the town. I hope you like the quiet life, my love. Because if you don't, then Riddler's Edge just isn't the place for you.'

'Oh, I dunno,' I said. 'Seems pretty exciting to me. I mean, I wasn't even off the train before there was a death.'

'My mother told me about that. The lady with the nut allergy. Such a lot of nut allergies, these days.'

'Are there?' I certainly hadn't been made aware of a lot of cases of death by peanut.

'Oh, yes.' He nodded knowingly. 'My mother, Norma, takes that train up and back from Dublin once a week like clockwork. There's been three unfortunate incidents on the train recently. Four now, if you include the last one. People really need to read menus more carefully if they've got an allergy.'

9. To the Lighthouse

After an afternoon of being shown the workings of the Daily Riddler, I was thoroughly bored. Everyone there was nice enough, but they were all being just as cagey as Greg and Grace. When I asked about the other recent nut allergy deaths Norman had told me about, they'd been even cagier. I was beginning to think this wasn't a trial period at all. Perhaps at the end of the week some cheesy TV presenter would appear and tell me I'd been on a hidden camera show the whole time.

When I returned to the Vander Inn, Donald had left the establishment and returned to his own home. A home that was in some unspecified nearby location, just like Malachy's restaurant. Pru was out for the night, apparently, so I ate dinner alone in the dining room, while Nollaig laid a large table for what she told me was a regular poker game.

'You're welcome to join us,' she said. 'We usually start around midnight and keep on until dawn.'

'Thanks, but I'm not much of a gambler.' I pushed my empty plate away. The meal had been lasagne and salad. Simple but delicious. Nollaig had made chocolate mousse for dessert, but I was too full to have it just yet. 'I might just head on up to my room. I had an early start this morning, so I'll probably be asleep before my head hits the pillow.'

Nollaig smiled. 'Whatever you like. We'll keep the noise to a minimum.'

≈

I'd fallen in love at first sight with my room. Turned out I was now falling in love at second sight, too. I raced to my bed, kicked off my boots, and pulled my phone from my bag.

I'd love to be able to tell you that I had a large array of friends to call and keep up to date. But when you move around as much as I did as a kid, you learn not to get close. And just like my reluctance to accumulate too many belongings, I'd continued to keep people at a distance long after I left foster care.

There was another reason I was eagerly looking at my mobile phone, and the reason was that I was a big fat liar.

Yeah, I liked to write things shorthand in my little reporter's notebook. I didn't write down what people *said* in there, though. I only jotted down general impressions. But I *did* record what people said, just not in my notebook – I used my mobile phone instead.

So yes, I'd lied to Greg about the notebook. I didn't like being sneaky and underhanded (okay, maybe just a little bit), but I needed to throw him off guard. If he didn't think I was recording anything, then he wouldn't have any reason to try and sabotage my mobile phone.

And no, I didn't consider him above sabotage. I knew I'd done the right thing in secretly recording things throughout my day. And now that I was finally alone, it was time to find out – was I paranoid, or was this whole town out to get me?

I played back my conversation with Miriam, stopping and rewinding, over and over, at the point where she said, 'I mean, Gunnar *looks* shady I know, what with the Vlad's Boys tattoo and everything. But I hope he's not really like that. He couldn't be, could he? Not deep down. He's probably just easily led. He would never have killed–'

No, I wasn't paranoid. Miriam had said exactly what I remembered her saying, word for word. I listened to some more snippets from my first day in Riddler's Edge, confirming that pretty much *everything* had been as weird as I'd thought at the time.

But where was that going to get me? What was I supposed to *do* with any of this? Did they want me to figure out the town's secrets by myself, and pass the trial that way? Or did they want me to prove I could shut up and take directions? I sighed. I'd *never* been one to shut up and take directions. And what sort of editor would want a reporter who *didn't* butt in where they weren't wanted? I mean, sure, that was exactly what John had wanted at the Daily Dubliner, but not every editor could be that short-sighted. Could they?

I took a stroll towards the French doors, and trained the telescope on the lighthouse. Detective Quinn's car was there, and there were lights on inside. My eyes widened. No. No way in the world could *he* live at the lighthouse. He had to be there for some other reason. Like … he was just *visiting* the sexy barefoot man who did carpentry in his spare time.

I gritted my teeth. He did live there. I knew it the same way I knew Monday was the longest day of the week. I knew it the same way I knew I'd never look good in hot-pants. And that whole thing I said about lighthouses being sexy? Well, maybe I was changing my mind. I mean, they were just tall, skinny, badly proportioned buildings. Nothing alluring about them at all.

Anyway, it didn't matter *why* the detective's car was parked at the lighthouse. The point was, if his car was there, he was there. I'd been keeping my mouth zipped for hours now, and I was sick of it. It was time to start behaving like myself, and get the answers I wanted. And who better to give them to me than the man who had the same mysterious condition as Bathsheba?

I glanced at my watch. It was just after seven, and the light was fading fast. I should have hired a car for the journey to Riddler's Edge, but I'd always hated driving. I was never quite sure *how* I passed my driving test. Any time I had to drive for work in Dublin I'd done so in an automatic, and even that was dicey.

Still, I thought as I pulled my boots on again, a walk in the dark couldn't be all that bad. Not when I had a lighthouse to guide my way.

≈

Halfway along the road, I realised that a no-longer-operational lighthouse *isn't* much good at guiding the way, so I pulled my little torch from my bag and switched it on. The closer I drew to the lighthouse, though, the less my torch seemed to see. I banged it about a few times, pulled the battery out and put it back in again. I tried the torch app on my mobile phone, too, but I still couldn't see more than a foot in front of me.

Somewhere in the near-distance, I could hear noise picking up. There was a line of trees on the horizon, a line I hadn't noticed earlier on – maybe those trees were what was covered by the haze? The noise seemed to be coming from there. Voices were chatting and laughing. Something was howling. Seriously? Howling?

'I feel the need to swear,' I muttered. 'The *very* strong need to swear. And then to flee. To flee while swearing profusely.'

I banged a few more times at my torch, and even switched the battery out for the spare one I kept in my purse, but the new one seemed to be totally fried.

'I'm not giving up,' I said, muttering again. Hey, I was hearing things, seeing things, and still convinced that almost everyone in town was holding out on me, so I might as well talk to myself, too. 'I'm *going* to that lighthouse.'

As soon as I said it, the beam on my torch began to work. 'Well, would you look at that?' I gave myself a self-congratulatory pat on the shoulder, and picked up my pace. As I neared the lighthouse, though, I paused again. I had to, because … wow.

Okay, so I know that you totally bought that whole thing about me no longer finding lighthouses sexy. I also know that you'll be *completely* surprised to read that I was having a sudden and profound turnaround on that thought.

I was in love with this place. Truly, madly, deeply. There was no point in denying it anymore. This really was the house of my fantasies. It was just a pity about the guy inside.

I only had one foot on the shingle driveway when Detective Quinn yanked open the front door and shouted out, 'Who the hell is there? Show yourself or I'll shoot.'

Yip, there he was – the man I loathed.

'It's me, Detective Quinn,' I said. 'Ash. Aisling Smith.'

He was illuminated in his doorway, standing a little back from the threshold. In his hands he carried a pair of sunglasses. I had an amazing view of him. So amazing that I could see the way his lip curled as soon as he heard my voice.

'For the love of the goddess,' he said. 'And there was me thinking you couldn't possibly get any more annoying. Listen, I'm off duty. Whatever you have to say, you can say it at the garda station tomorrow.'

I made my way up the shingle driveway and stood in his view. 'I would do, if I thought it'd make a difference. No, I think I'll say it to you *now*. Where's Gunnar Lucien, Detective Quinn?'

His sawed his jaw. 'He's in the land of none of your business. It's just adjacent to the land of get the hell off my property.' He moved further back inside, and slammed the door.

Here's the thing. You might not have noticed it yet, but I really am a stubborn person. Some say I'm stubborn to a fault, but I say I'm stubborn to a purpose. So I did what any stubborn to a purpose woman would do. I banged on his door and shouted through his letterbox. 'What's Vlad's Boys, Detective Quinn?'

No answer.

'What's this condition you've got, Detective Quinn? Something similar to Bathsheba Brookes? Last I heard, you couldn't *contract* a nut allergy. What's with the sunglasses after dark? What's with the lies? What's with this whole godforsaken *town*?'

He ripped open the door. Oh my. I hadn't noticed the first time he opened the door, but he was barefoot. A barefoot, dark-haired man in a lighthouse.

I really wished his toes could have been weird. Not because I have a fetish for weird toes (but each to their own). More because I wished that this man had at least one flaw in his appearance. He had plenty in his personality, though, so I guess that would have to do.

'Come in before you wake the whole town up, you crazy witch!'

≈

Well, it didn't exactly help to discover that inside the lighthouse was even better than outside. The kitchen had the perfect blend of old and new – natural wood countertops mixed with modern appliances. The living room was *circular* for criminy's sake. Not *shag-pad* circular like Grace's apartment. More *statement interior design* circular.

There was a spiral staircase at the side of the room, and I could see a lit-up deck outside, leading all the way down to the beach.

Gulp.

There were a few photos on the walls and on a shelf by the TV. All of them featured a woman with chestnut hair, sallow skin and dark brown eyes. In some she was kissing Detective Quinn. In others she was smiling coyly at the camera. In *all* of them she looked amazing. And in the ones where she was wearing hot-pants? Well, I guess some women really do have it all. Maybe if I did more lunges and squats I'd have thighs like that. Did I say *more* lunges and squats? I should have said any.

'She your wife?' I asked.

'She's none of your business is who she is.'

'Wow,' I said. 'You *definitely* belie the myth that people in small Irish towns are friendly. You also belie the myth that we don't pay our public servants enough. This place must have cost a fortune.'

He rolled his eyes. 'I inherited the lighthouse. Not that it's any of your business. Not that *any* of this is any of your business. For some reason I can't quite work out, Arnold decided to give you a trial. But trust me, a trial is all it's ever going to be. You're not cut out for this place.'

'Really?' I sat down into a squishy couch, trying to appear casual. 'I'm not cut out for a tiny town that's going through a mysterious spate of nut-allergy related deaths? Well, it's a good thing I wasted all those years training as an investigative journalist, then.'

He narrowed his eyes. 'What did you just say?'

'Which part? The part where I said I was an investigative journalist or the part where I said *a spate.* Well, yeah. I'd call four deaths in as many weeks a spate. Wouldn't you?'

He moved into the kitchen, and I shuffled around in the seat so I could watch him. He was at the coffee machine, pouring himself a small shot of espresso.

'Yes, please,' I said.

'I didn't offer you one.'

'Oh, I know – but I thought I might just help your manners along. Detective Quinn, I've been a journalist for over eight years. I've travelled to plenty of small towns to ask questions when there's been a murder. Never one as small as *this,* mind you. But the funny thing is, very few of those places had a permanent detective in their station. Few of them even *had* a station anymore, thanks to cutbacks. So how come Riddler's Edge has its very own detective?' I glanced at the holster on his back. The holster that was accentuating his toned physique a little more than I would like. 'Do you find you *need* to use your gun a lot around here?'

He fixed a second espresso and carried them both over, setting them on the coffee table. 'You ask a lot of questions for a reporter on a small town paper,' he said. 'You know you're only going to be writing about school fairs and the church choir's latest fundraiser, right? And that's *if* you get the job. This isn't the big city, Miss Smith. There's no major crime here. Today a woman died because she didn't bother to ask if there were going to be nuts in her muesli. That's right. I said muesli. Because that's what Bathsheba had to eat. This is a silly, senseless death. But it's not a murder.'

I picked up my coffee and sipped. Then I pushed it away, and decided that one sip would have to do. It wasn't bad – quite the opposite. But if I was going to keep on disliking this man, then the last thing I needed was his delicious coffee in my hands to sway my decision. Just to make sure I drove the message completely home, I glanced at the photos. Because if there was anything that was going to turn me off a man, then it was the knowledge that he was already attached.

'You can stop with the formality,' I said. 'Call me Ash. Oh, and you can stop with the obfuscations, too. You keep talking around me, swerving a hundred miles from the subject, not actually answering any of my questions. And by the way, I sat with Bathsheba in the dining car. She did *not* have any muesli.'

He knocked back his coffee and stood up, crossing the room and pulling on a pair of shoes that were sitting by some sliding doors. 'Like I told you earlier on, I'll include any information that the newspaper needs to know in my report. Now come on, I'm driving you home. There are no lights along the road back into town. I don't know how you got here without falling into a ditch.'

I pulled my torch from my bag and waved it in the air. 'I used this crazy new invention to find my way here, so I think I can use it again on the way back.'

His eyes seemed to be looking in far too much interest at my torch. Maybe the cutbacks in An Garda Síochána were even worse than I thought. The poor things weren't even given torches these days, judging by the look of confusion on his face.

'You … used a torch?' he asked.

'I did. And like I said, I'm perfectly capable of using it again. I mean don't get me wrong, I was a *little* put out by the howls coming from that forest over yonder. But I can always stick my headphones on to drown them out.' I gave him a tight smile, stood up, and prepared to leave. 'I'll look forward to your report, Detective Quinn. I'm sure it'll be totally uninformative, just like every conversation we've had so far.'

I had just reached my hand towards the front door, when I felt his palm wrap around my wrist.

10. Can't See the Woods for the Mist

'What did you just say?' he asked, his voice intense, his eyes blazing.

I shook his hand away. 'I would have thought that a garda detective would be aware it's *not* appropriate to go grabbing onto women out of the blue. And you heard perfectly well what I said.'

As I pulled open the door, he stood back in the shadows. 'Please, Miss Smith. I apologise for grabbing onto your wrist. I just … I thought you said you saw the forest. Which forest? The one to the south of the church?'

'No. The one to the north of *here*.'

The intense look still hadn't left his eyes. 'Maybe Arnold was right about one of you, at last. Wait a second, will you? Please. I want to show you something.'

I thought about it for a second or two. Sure, I hated this guy with a ridiculously deep loathing. But I did want answers, and whatever I'd said about the woods seemed to be cracking his exterior. 'Fine. But hurry up. I want to get an early night.'

He rushed to the coat stand and pulled on a hooded sweater, wrapped a scarf around his face, slipped his hands into gloves, then popped on his sunglasses. 'I … I think I'm coming down with a cold,' he said. 'You can never be too careful.'

'Sure.' I arched a brow. 'A cold. I mean, if it weren't for the sunglasses it might almost be convincing.' I marched towards his car, and he opened the door with a button on his keyring. Quite right, too. I mean, it wasn't as though I would have preferred him to open the door himself. This wasn't the fifties. I mean, it sure seemed like the fifties in the Daily Riddler office, but you know what I mean.

The car turned out to have an automatic gearbox. My many short-lived relationships had told me that Irish guys preferred manual transmissions. But Detective Quinn wasn't exactly the typical Irish guy. He sped a little past the lighthouse, then took the left turn that I'd seen him take earlier. By now, we were in a heavily wooded area, on a dirt road only wide enough for one car.

'You still see the forest?' he asked.

'Yeah, I do,' I answered. As soon as I said it, though, I shook my head and took another look out the window. A second ago, tall trees had been everywhere. Now, all I could see was mist. 'Um … revise my earlier statement,' I said. 'It's gotten so misty now that I can't see a thing.'

He stopped the car, right there in the middle of the dirt road. 'You see mist? Right now?' He scratched his chin. 'No forest anymore?'

I looked away from him. The way he was acting made me fear I might be in the middle of a mental health intervention. But I knew what I'd seen before, and I knew what I saw right now. First, there was that far too familiar kaleidoscope-haze over this area. Then there was forest. Now there was mist.

'And your torch?' he pressed. 'It didn't … act up? Along the road to my house?'

I resisted the urge to turn to him and scream *What the heck?* Every word he uttered was proving to me that I wasn't some paranoid conspiracy nut. And just as I felt surer of that fact than I *ever* had before, a buzzing sensation began to work its way through me. Something *was* going on in this town. Something big. Something that Detective Quinn knew all about.

I turned in my seat. 'I think you know more about my torch than I do,' I said. 'I think you know more about *everything* than I do. So why not just spit it out, Detective?'

He let out a sigh. 'I … the thing is … well … this is a *trial,* Miss Smith. It's up to Arnold to tell you all of this if you get the job.'

'Oh my God!' I held my hands up, and a grunt of frustration escaped. 'Look, if you're not going to tell me where Gunnar is, then for the love of God, tell me what is *up* with the outfit.' As I heard the words come out of my mouth, I had a sudden recollection of something Detective Quinn said when I arrived. 'Wait a minute. When I got to your place, you said "*For the love of the goddess.*" I've heard that before. From you earlier, sure, but from other people, too. I was interviewing people about some murders in Dublin last summer. Weird murders. Murders that the gardaí in Dublin palmed off with some stupid excuse. A stupid excuse like the one *you're* trying to get me to buy right now.'

I got the sense that, behind those sunglasses, he was blinking rapidly. 'I don't … I can't … look, do you actually *remember* these weird murders? Do you remember people using phrases like "For the love of the goddess"?'

'Of course I remember. A guy killed an old woman in St Stephen's Green with a tennis racket, and a candle shop owner was murdered *with* a candlestick. Who wouldn't remember a thing like that? Although I'm sure you're the sort of sexist jerk who'd like to think all women have brains like sieves, we *don't.*'

'I'm not sexist. Why would you say I'm sexist?'

'Oh, gee, I wonder now … would it be because you've been treating me like a great big dummy all day? Or calling me Miss Smith? Or refusing to answer a single question I've asked, because why should you have to answer the dumb blonde's questions? Oh, or maybe it was because you thought it was perfectly okay to just cop a feel of me without even asking first?'

His mouth opened and closed a few times, with no words escaping. Eventually there was a strangled sound, followed by, 'I did *not* cop a feel. If I was going to cop a feel, I can think of parts of your body a *lot* more interesting than your wrists.' He scooted closer to his door and looked away. 'Okay, that didn't come out quite the way I meant. This is getting a bit out of hand. How about you tell me a little bit about yourself? Arnold said you grew up in the care system. Did you ever try to find your birth parents?'

I stared at him, feeling like I'd been kicked in the stomach. 'Arnold told you personal things about me? How dare he? And come to think of it, how dare any of you? How dare *any* of you in this stupid town? You're all treating me like some sort of idiot, and I'm getting a bit sick of it.' I turned to open the door.

Beside me, I heard him curse beneath his breath. 'Okay, so I want to grab your wrist and stop you from getting out of here right now. But I'm afraid you'll throw another fit if I do. So can I just ask you in a not at all sexist way to *please* stay in the car?'

There was something akin to panic in his voice. Slightly nearer to us than I would have liked, I heard another howl. I leant forward and peeked out through the windscreen. 'Somewhere up there beyond the mist,' I said, 'I have the feeling that there's a full moon in the sky.'

He nodded. 'You're right about that. Tonight is, most definitely, a full moon.'

I turned to him. 'I tell you what. Either you tell me everything, right now, or else I get out of this car and walk off into that mist. I mean, it shouldn't be a problem, right? Because there's nothing *weird* out there, is there? There's nothing weird in this town at all.'

I heard a clunking sound. He had locked the doors of the car. 'I can't let you do that, Miss Smith. Not tonight.' He sighed. 'I'm going to reach across you now. There's something in the glove box that I want to give you. Please don't mistake my actions for trying to cop a feel.'

I pressed my body back against my seat, and he opened the glove box. Inside there was a flask, a pair of gloves, another pair of sunglasses, and a small, velvet-covered box. He pulled it out and opened it up. A ring was sitting there. It was gold with a green stone at its centre.

I grinned at him. 'Well, it's a bit soon, Detective Quinn. And I mean, we're not even on a first name basis yet. But sure.' I held my left hand out. 'I'll marry you.'

'Put the ring on, Miss Smith,' he said with a mirthless laugh. 'When you do, we'll see where we go from there.'

I slipped the ring on, talking as I did so. 'Well, I don't know where *you* want to go, but I'm thinking a tour of wedding venues will do the trick. And of course we'll need to test all the menus within our budget. I'll want your advice on the bridesmaids' dresses too. And the …' I let my voice trail off. Outside the window, the mist had lifted. Once again, I could see the woods. Not only could I see the woods, but I could see the enormous wolf crossing the road.

A wolf? In Ireland? We hadn't had wolves for centuries.

I looked up at the moon and, as I did, something else caught my eye. There were lights through the trees. Lots of them. I sat forward and looked more carefully.

'There's a town over there,' I said. I turned to look at him. At some stage whilst I'd been babbling, he'd slipped a bracelet around his gloved wrist. One with an identical green stone as the one in my ring. 'I checked out the map of the local area before I came here,' I went on. 'There *is* no town close to Riddler's Edge. Not for miles.'

He shrugged. 'I think you're learning by now that maps don't tell the whole truth, Miss Smith. Arnold told me about the notebook you hide in your desk. The one with the list of non-existent place names. Lupin Lane? Luna Park? Eile Street? They all exist, Miss Smith. And so does that town. It's called Riddler's Cove.' He took a deep breath.

'Grace is going to have my guts for garters. But what the heck.' He started up the engine. 'Let's go for a drink.'

11. Riddler's Cove

No wonder I'd heard such a racket from this forest. It wasn't just the wolves out tonight. We passed at least half a dozen groves where people were circling with their hands held, chanting words I couldn't make out.

'Aren't they afraid of the wolves?'

Detective Quinn snorted. 'They're witches. A werewolf wouldn't dare attack them.'

I turned in my seat. 'So … you're being serious here?'

He kept his eyes on the narrow road ahead. 'You already know the answer to that, I suspect. A woman who's been keeping a log of odd events all these years should hardly be surprised to find out there's a whole other world. Yeah, those groups were witches, out for their full moon coven rituals. Those wolves were werewolves, also out enjoying the full moon. This town we're about to arrive in is a witch enclave, but other supernaturals are welcome. Well, these days, anyway.' He waved his wrist, nodding to the green-stoned bracelet. 'As long as we wear some special jewellery, we can gain entry.'

'Enclave?' I asked. It seemed like the safest question.

'It's … it's a sub-dimensional region. Kind of thing. Only supernaturals can see them – and like I said, this one is a *witch* enclave, so it's even better hidden than most. I mean, you'd be better off asking Greg to explain it. Wizards know a lot more about this stuff than I do.' He pulled into an empty parking space on the edge of the town. I couldn't see any other cars around. 'Come on. I'll take you to Three Witches Brew if you promise not to gawk. You're going to need a drink for all of this.'

He didn't wait for me to answer. He just locked the car and began to walk towards the entranceway of a thatched-roof building.

The place was quiet inside, with just a few people sitting around drinking and chatting. I'm not sure what he thought I was going to gawk at, because everyone looked just as human as I did. Sure, there was a woman who seemed to be making a bottle of wine refill her glass without actually *touching* the bottle. If she was a witch then she was a show-off, too. How hard was it to lift a bottle?

'She just got her power,' Detective Quinn whispered as he took off his sunglasses and pulled down his hood. 'It came a few days after her nineteenth birthday, so you can't really blame her for celebrating. Twenty-one is the cut-off point for witches, and most get their power when they're kids, so she was over the moon when hers finally arrived.'

The young woman waved at him and smiled, as did all of her female friends. 'Hey, Detective Yummy!' the girl called over as he made his way to the bar.

'Hey, Chantelle,' he called back. 'Have a good evening. Don't do anything I wouldn't do.'

She giggled and turned back to her friends, who were all furiously whispering, giggling, and casting not-so-surreptitious glances in the detective's direction.

'Speaking of staying safe,' he said, oblivious to the table of young women who were clearly enamoured with him, 'I never drink and drive, so I'll be having a soft drink tonight. But you should try a Superbrew.'

'It can't exactly make the night any weirder, so why not?'

The barman seemed to know him, and they chatted while our drinks were prepared. His hair was even blacker than the detective's, a feat I hadn't thought possible, and he had shining grey eyes that made him look friendly and alert. With my tankard of oddness in hand, I followed the detective to a booth at the back of the bar.

'Okay,' he said. 'What do you want to know?'

'I want to know why you arrested that kid. Gunnar. That's what I really want to know. Did he murder Bathsheba?'

He gave me a funny smile. 'You do realise most people would ask a million questions about this new and wonderful world they've just been admitted to? There's a lot that I really should explain before we get into talking about the murder.'

I shrugged. 'Sure, I want to know all that. But first I want to know about Gunnar.'

He sat back, sipping his cola. 'Fine. You saw the tattoo on his neck? Vlad's Boys? Well, to say that they're elitists would be putting it mildly. They hate dayturning vampires. Which is why I arrested Gunnar. He had motive *and* opportunity.'

'Wait … Bathsheba was a dayturning vampire? What's that when it's at home?'

He rolled his eyes. He did that an awful lot around me, for some reason. 'I told you I needed to explain the background first, but you wouldn't listen. Bathsheba was a vampire for almost three hundred years, but she and her husband didn't become vampires until they were in their eighties. Bathsheba had an incurable illness, and Donald couldn't bear the thought of life without her. He became a vampire, and turned her into one, too.'

I gasped. 'That's so romantic!'

The detective rolled his eyes. 'Romantic? Yeah, right. Death happens, Miss Smith. Donald and Bathsheba had already had decades together when they turned. They weren't being romantic. They were being selfish.'

'Gee, you're just a little ray of sunshine, aren't you? Fine, let's agree to disagree. I know what a vampire is – or I think I do, anyway. You still haven't told me what a dayturning vampire is, though.'

A dark look passed over his face. It was clearly a sore subject for him. 'A while ago, Bathsheba bought some blood from a bad batch and contracted the dayturner virus.' He swallowed. 'It's a mutated form of the vampire virus. The darkness that vampires love so much becomes unbearable, giving the infected vampire a painful, incurable rash should they dare to venture out at night. Feeding at night is a no-go, too. Serious indigestion. So when morning comes, they're crazy hungry. The virus supposedly originated by bad turning practices – not taking your first feed from the vampire who turned you – but it's changing all the time. Tainted blood flooded the market a while back and ... well ... it's becoming a bit of a problem.'

He was doing his best to avoid my eyes. 'So that's why Bathsheba was on the train wearing sunglasses and all the rest? Because it was still dark outside when she got on?'

He cleared his throat. 'Yes. That's why. It was Night potion that killed her, not a nut allergy. It mimics the effect of darkness on a dayturning vampire, but intensifies it a hundredfold. The rash and the boils, the quick and painful death that Bathsheba experienced … it was because of the potion. Night potion is a horrific poison, and Vlad's Boys have been taking the credit for dozens of such murders in recent weeks. Bathsheba's was the fourth murder to take place on the Riddler's Express.'

So Norman was right about the spate. It just happened to be caused by a poison instead of a nut allergy. It was bad enough that these dayturning vampires couldn't go out at night. But to have someone feed them a poison that affected them in the same way that the darkness would, only quicker? I shivered. I'd never been one of those vampire fan-girls, the kind who dream of a pointy-toothed lover who longs for their blood. But I'd spoken to Bathsheba. She seemed like a lovely woman. Whatever she was, she didn't deserve to die that way.

I looked at the detective. 'So … you're a dayturner too?'

He gave me a tight smile. 'As of very recently. And no, I won't relate the story of how I came to be that way. There's … there's been no government funding for a while, but supposedly that's about to change. There are some people working to find a cure at the moment, of course. Some charitable organisations and some private healing facilities. No one seems close. Bathsheba, myself and some others on the train were on our way back from a course of treatment at Night and Gale when she was killed. There were two humans on the train – you and Norma. I *am* a garda detective, and I do work on human cases, too. But any time something supernatural comes up in town, it's my job to clear it up with the help of the Wayfarers – the supernatural police. Like Gretel, who you sat beside on the train. So she and I had to go through a bit of a charade. Come up with a plausible excuse. Use certain techniques to make sure the humans bought what we were selling. Except that you didn't. Normally, we'd just perform a memory spell on a human who asks too many questions.'

'But instead you let me bug the hell out of you. Why? Because Arnold hired me?'

He looked up at me. 'Yes. Except … except that this is just a trial, Miss Smith. Grace and me, we didn't think it was going to work out. We thought … we thought your memory *would* be wiped at the end of it.'

I stared at him. 'You're serious? You were going to wipe my memory?'

He looked into his glass. 'Not me. Arnold. Look, I think it's been a bit obvious that I was never keen on you being in Riddler's Edge.' He clenched his jaw. 'Arnold … Arnold has his reasons, and I get that. But until tonight, I was so angry with him for bringing you here. You don't seem supernatural. And yet here you are. Seeing things you shouldn't be able to. Turning up at my lighthouse without your torch going haywire. My lighthouse is on a boundary line, Miss Smith. Riddler's *Cove* is the supernatural area. Riddler's Edge has a lot of supernatural residents, even an enclave or two on the outskirts, but it's not, on the whole, a magical town. The town receives a little accidental overflow from Riddler's Cove from time to time, but for the most part it's … well, normal.'

My head was beginning to ache. 'Wait. *This* place is the witchy town, a town that humans *can't* see. Riddler's Edge, the place where *nothing* normal has happened since my arrival, *isn't* supernatural? It's what, some sort of boundary town?'

He nodded. 'Yeah, pretty much. Like I said, there are a lot of supernatural residents, but the main areas of Riddler's Edge are on the map, and fully accessible to humans. *This* town we're in right now, it isn't on any map a human would be able to see. My lighthouse is the last point before the non-magical world ends, and the magical one begins. There are certain discouragements in place, should anyone get that far. Cars break down, unless they're specifically designed for the area – as mine is. Torches, mobile phones … these things *shouldn't* work when a human gets too close to the boundary. Everything about my lighthouse should have made you turn away this evening. Lighthouses in the human world are designed to show people the way. Mine is designed to send them running the *other* way.'

I took a sip of my Superbrew. It tasted herby and intoxicating, so I took a few more sips while I mulled over what he'd told me. If he wanted to turn people away, then maybe he shouldn't live in such a sexy building. Did I just think that? Clearly it was the drink doing the thinking.

'Once we actually entered the woods, you couldn't see them without a Ring of Privilege. But ... you could see *something.* I have the feeling you've been catching glimpses of the supernatural world for a very long time. I'm starting to think that maybe Arnold was right to hire you, after all.'

'Wow,' I said, slurping yet more of my drink. 'I feel so validated now. I totally forgive all of you for considering messing with my memories.'

He snorted. 'Anyway. Like I said, Gunnar is the only suspect. End of. Vlad's Boys have already claimed responsibility for dozens of dayturner murders. Gunnar is in a supernatural prison right now, and he's not answering any of our questions. But I think we can build a pretty strong case.'

I looked down into my tankard, wondering where the rest of my Superbrew had gone. I missed it already. It made me feel happy, strong and ready for anything. 'Okay,' I said. 'Thanks for telling me. Hey, how about I go buy us another round of drinks? Because I don't know if you've noticed, but I'm a bit of a curious cat. I have a lot more questions.'

He groaned. 'I'll just bet you do. But let me buy the next round. You won't have the kind of currency they take in this place.'

12. Fuzz

The poker game was off to a start by the time I returned to the Vander Inn. I looked briefly in to say hello, but I went up to bed soon afterwards. Partially because I wanted to be well-rested for the morning, but also because I knew I'd spend the entire game staring at people and trying to figure out what kind of supernatural they were.

Detective Quinn had told me more during our second drink and on the short drive home. But I felt like there was so much he was holding back. Sure, I now knew that there was actually such a thing as a weredog, and that wizards were a whole different thing to witches.

I also knew that my hosts – Nollaig and Pru – were vampires. I probably should have been more put off by that, but surprisingly I wasn't. I liked Pru and her mother instinctively, and I was pretty sure that if they *did* want to suck my blood, that they'd at least ask politely first.

But I was still confused about Detective Quinn. He talked about becoming a dayturner recently. But he was a member of this community long before.

And he lived in a lighthouse that was on the boundary between Riddler's Edge and Riddler's Cove, so he *must* have been supernatural already. Right?

More importantly than any of that, though, I couldn't help but wonder why Arnold hired me in the first place. I was the fourth reporter on trial here, and none of the others had worked out. The odds were that I wouldn't, either. Which meant that, come Friday, Arnold was going to try to turn my brain to Swiss cheese. I was feeling more than a little angry about that.

With so many thoughts running through my mind, I thought I'd never drop off – but I hadn't taken the most comfortable bed in the world into account. It was like sleeping on a cloud. Actually, a cloud might be a little bit damp and porous. Maybe a marshmallow? When I woke I felt more refreshed than I had in … ever. All I wanted to do was skip along to the Daily Riddler and demand a meeting with Arnold.

Just as I was getting dressed, though, I noticed something lying on an armchair in the corner of the room. Something that hadn't been there before. 'Hey there, kitty,' I said as I walked towards the sleeping black cat. I glanced around the room. The doors were firmly closed, as were all the windows. 'How did you get in here?'

The cat raised its head, and peered at me through yellow-green eyes. It began to purr, and jumped down off the chair and brushed itself against my legs. I picked it up and began to stroke the lustrous black fur – on further examination, it was definitely a *he.* I kept him in my arms as I walked downstairs. He was so warm and fluffy that I wished I could keep him in my arms forever. But no doubt he belonged to Nollaig or Pru, and he'd just gotten stuck in my room last night when I tipsily closed the door without noticing him there.

Pru was laying the table for breakfast when I entered. 'Hey Ash,' she said, smiling. 'Mam's just gone up to bed for the day. I mean … because she's sick. Hey, who's your little friend?'

The cat meowed.

'He's not yours?' I asked. 'I found him in my room.'

Pru shook her head. She was dressed in what I was coming to think of as her usual uniform – a gypsy shirt and jeans, and a lot of silver jewellery. 'Never seen him before in my life. Cats tend to stay away from us. Because … um …'

'It's okay.' I sat at the table with the cat on my lap. 'I know you're vampires. Although I'm confused about why you've all been keeping it a secret – seeing as Arnold's probably going to wipe my memory on Friday.'

Pru's eyes widened, and she dropped into a seat opposite me. 'He's going to what now?'

She seemed genuinely surprised, even a little angry. 'Well, that's what he's done with the previous reporters he's trialled – according to Detective Quinn anyway.'

Pru scrunched up her nose. 'You know we all just call him Dylan, right? We're not very formal around here. But honestly, Ash, I had no idea that's what happened to the previous reporters. Any time Arnold asked us to put one up, he asked us to keep shtum on what we were until they got comfortable. He said he wanted to break things to them gently or whatever. And when they didn't stay on, I figured they'd just decided the place was too weird for them.'

'Yeah, that's not what happened.' I reached for a slice of toast and began to butter it, thinking carefully. Why was Arnold asking the supernatural residents to keep their true nature a secret if I was going to be forced to forget I ever even met them? 'But don't worry about it. You only did what you were asked. Hey, I'm not really sure what to do about this gorgeous guy then, if he's not yours?' I stroked the cat. 'Should I try to find his owner? Or feed him? I've never had a pet, so I really have no clue.'

Pru shrugged and poured herself some juice. 'We'll leave the window in the kitchen open so he can come and go as he wants – although, I really did mean it when I said that cats tend not to like me and my mam, so it's super weird that he's here in the first place. I'll leave out some food for him and, I dunno, maybe put up a sign in the shop? See if someone is missing him? But you know what cats are like. The place they are is usually the place they want to be.'

≈

I arrived early at the Daily Riddler, but the door was open so I knew I wasn't the first. When I strode towards the desk that had been allotted to me, I spied Edward, the cleaner, and Roarke, the guy who wrote the puzzles. For some reason, the two of them were hiding under the desk adjacent to mine.

'Hi guys,' I said. 'Something interesting down there?'

Edward put a finger to his lips, while Roarke pointed towards the staircase. A moment later, I heard the sound of something crashing in Grace's apartment. Another moment passed before I heard angry shouting. It sounded like Grace and Detective Quinn.

'How long have they been at it?' I whispered.

'Half an hour,' Edward whispered back. 'Although I was running the vacuum cleaner for a while so it could be even longer. I didn't see Dylan arrive.'

'I think it's about you,' said Roarke.

As if to underline his assertion, I suddenly heard Grace scream, 'And what am I supposed to do about Aisling *now*?'

'I reckon you might be right,' I said. 'Are Malachy and Greg up there too?'

Roarke shook his head. 'They were,' he whispered. 'But now Greg's pretending to fix something in the server room, and Malachy's off making everyone some chamomile tea.'

I sat at my desk and turned on my computer, thinking that I might take this chance to get a better look at the newspaper's private network. Greg had told me it was down, but given everything I'd learned last night, I was pretty sure he was lying. Just as I managed to navigate myself as far as the password screen, I heard my name screamed aloud once again.

Decision time. I could sit here and try to sneak my way past Greg's network security (and, let's face it, I was *never* going to manage that), or I could go up there and demand a password. Actually, I could go up there and demand a lot more than just a password.

I didn't think on it too long, in case I talked myself out of it – instead I threw my bag on my desk, marched up the stairs and knocked loudly on Grace's door.

'I can tell that you're both *really* enjoying your little tiff,' I called out. 'But seeing as I've heard my name mentioned a dozen or so times, I figure this might be something I ought to be in on.'

The shouts lowered to intense whispers, and then Grace pulled open the door. 'You can come in,

Ash,' she said. She turned to the detective. 'And you, Dylan, can most definitely get out.'

He scowled at her and left the apartment, not even looking my way as he thundered down the stairs and out of the building.

Grace moved to her desk, tossing back her hair and doing her best to appear composed. 'Look,' she said. 'Dylan should *never* have brought you to Riddler's Cove last night. No matter how many trees you saw.' She picked up the same magnifying glass she had peered through yesterday, and handed it to me. 'This is an Aurameter. It allows me to see if a person is a witch or not. I can see their power through it. It's like … this enormous aura surrounding them. If the person is a powerful witch, then looking through this should almost blind you. If they're your average, work-a-day witch, then you'll see a nice golden glow surrounding them. If they're without power, well then … you'll just see their pores.' She shrugged her shoulders. 'And I'm afraid that all I could see when I looked at you were pores.'

I picked it up and raised it to my left eye, looking at Grace. Then I dropped it, shook my head, and picked it up again. No, I hadn't been imagining it the first time – Grace was surrounded by a line of gold. It was stunning.

I could hear chatter downstairs – it sounded like Malachy and Greg. They must have come out of hiding after the detective left.

I rushed to the stairs, the Aurameter in my hands, and peered through it at them both. They were standing around with Edward and Roarke, probably talking about what was going on upstairs. There was nothing to see, though, when I looked at Malachy and Greg. I might as well have been looking through an average magnifying glass. I looked at Edward and Roarke next. Edward had no glow, either, but Roarke had a faint golden shimmer.

I could hear Grace rush out after me. 'What are you doing?' She snapped the Aurameter from my hands. 'You can't *make* yourself have power, Ash, much as you want to. And whilst I might not care about anything except the fact that you're a decent reporter, Arnold isn't *looking* for a decent reporter. He's looking for … for something else.' She flounced back to her desk and I followed, sitting across from her.

'Okay, I'll be asking you about what it is that Arnold wants in just a second,' I said. 'But first – how come Greg and Malachy don't have the same golden glow as you? Oh, yeah – Greg's a wizard, right? His power isn't innate. Or something. But what kind of supernatural is Malachy? Or is that a rude question?'

She blinked, her false lashes causing a bit of a butterfly effect. 'Excuse me?'

'I'm talking about what I saw when I looked through the Aurameter. You have the lovely golden glow you were talking about. Not blinding, but pretty fandabidozi if I do say so myself. But Greg and Malachy … well, I imagine if I was standing a bit closer, all I'd see was their pores. Roarke has something too, but it's fainter than your glow.'

She swallowed. 'You … you *see* through the Aurameter?'

'Isn't that what it's for?'

She swallowed again. 'Aisling … you … you *shouldn't* see through the Aurameter. Only an empowered witch can see through the Aurameter. And I'm telling you, you *have* no power. Like Dylan told you last night, Greg is a wizard. He gets his power from outside sources. Hence no glow. Malachy is a vampire. We need different devices to see their powers. Edward's a weredog, and they don't really *have* any powers other than howling at the moon and having a great sense of smell.' She paused. 'You definitely see a golden glow when you look at me and Roarke?'

'I definitely do. Much fainter with Roarke, though. What does that mean?'

She looked completely unsure. Of course, that was the exact moment that the cat decided to make appearance.

'Oh yeah,' I said. 'This cat turned up in my room this morning. Cute, isn't he? I think Pru's going to post an advert in the local shop to see if anyone's missing him, but maybe we could run something in the paper, too.'

She stared from the cat to me. Then she raised a finger, swirled it about, and magically closed the door to her apartment.

≈

Five minutes later, we were still locked inside her apartment together, and Grace had yet to say a thing. The closed door told me that she *wanted* to say something, though, so I figured I might as well just hang out with the cat and wait.

'You know …' she said after the sixth minute.

'It's just that …' she added after the seventh minute.

'Okay,' she said after ten minutes had passed. 'I'm just going to lay it out on the table. Dylan has explained why he told you what he told you last night. He told me you see a haze surrounding supernatural areas. Well, you shouldn't. That haze is what we refer to as a veil of mist spell. One of many methods we use to keep the entry points to our enclaves hidden from the world. It's the same haze that supernaturals who *aren't* witches sometimes see when they look upon a witch enclave without some form of Admitaz – that's the green stone in the ring you're wearing.'

'Oh.' I'd forgotten to take the ring off, and Detective Quinn had never asked for it back. 'Yeah, Detective Quinn said something about witch enclaves being different. Like, you need to be one of them, or to wear some magical jewellery to enter there.'

She nodded. 'Exactly. Now, you've met Dylan, so you know that there are also unempowered witches. Witches born to witch parents, but who don't have any power themselves.'

'He said he was a dayturner,' I interrupted.

'Ah. Yes. Well, now he is. But he was born an unempowered witch. And I had *you* pegged an unempowered witch, too. Right up until you told me you could see my power through the Aurameter. You got all of it spot on. I have an average amount of power, hence the golden glow. Roarke is just barely empowered, so his glow is far fainter. And you saw that. All of it. And now, of course, there's the matter of the cat.' She gave me a funny smile. 'Can you hear him, right now?'

I looked down at the black cat. He was looking up at me and purring. 'Yeah, he's like a little motorboat, isn't he? I see what people like about cats.'

Grace blinked. 'That's all you hear? Him purring? Because *I* hear him talking.' She looked at the cat. 'All right, I'll tell her.' She sighed and turned back to me. 'He says that there's no need to put any signs up. He told me that you are most definitely his. He also says to tell you his name is Fuzz. Not the most elegant name in the world, but …'

I gawped down at the cat. 'Fuzz?'

The cat nodded.

'And you've decided that I'm yours, have you?'

He nodded again.

'Ash, Dylan and I … we didn't want you here,' Grace went on, striding to her sunken couch and beckoning me to follow. 'We didn't want to run this trial, because we have already run three trials, with three other women hired by Arnold. And it didn't bother me that none of those women were witches. They were excellent journalists. It's *not* uncommon for humans to work in our world, as long as they know how to keep a secret. Whether you were an unempowered witch, or a human … no matter what you are, no matter what any of the other reporters were, it didn't matter to me. But it does matter to Arnold. He's looking for something specific. Some*one* specific. I think it's safe to say that you have some power, even if I can't see it through the Aurameter. But … I can't promise you that you'll be what Arnold is looking for. At the end of this week, he might still try to do his memory spell. You might forget all of this ever happened. I shall argue your case, of course, but … I'm not sure whether I'll be able to stop him.'

The cat had come over to the couch too, and I lifted him up, feeling somehow comforted by his presence. 'I'm not okay with that. But if you have magical powers and you still don't think you'll be able to stop Arnold, then there's probably not a lot I'll be able to do about it, either.'

Her eyes watered a little bit. 'No. Probably not. But in the meantime, I'd like to continue with this trial. I'd like you to do a real piece on Bathsheba's murder. A piece for the evening edition.'

13. The Evening Edition

On the surface of it, there was little difference between the Daily Riddler's daily and evening editions. They both covered the same stories, and they both included a *crazy* amount of puzzles.

But when you looked closer, you saw that the two were nothing alike. The whole job of the daily edition was to come up with an explanation for the strange things that happened in Riddler's Edge.

One story featured an explosion that took place on the beach. It had been caused by a wizard – a friend of Greg's, in fact – who underestimated the power of a magical shell he'd found on the strand. In the daily edition, the article talked about some careless tourist letting a camp fire get out of hand on the beach, whereas in the evening edition, the true story was told.

There were some differences in the word puzzles too, but that was just sensible. I can't imagine many humans would have known the answer to questions like: *It's a substitute for lurpwart in a popular cold remedy. It's also the name of a famous vampire opera singer.*

As well as finally letting me see the evening edition, Greg had given me the passwords for the paper's network. He'd also given me the password for the search engine that supernaturals accessed online. He gave me books to read, too, so I could swot up on the Irish supernatural world.

Once he got me acquainted with the real newspaper, we got to work on the story Grace had asked me to write. Greg showed me Grace's own reports on the previous Night potion murders, and how to pull up all the reports the detective had submitted. I read over every single word as many times as I could. Seeing as I was going to be questioning Gunnar Lucien the next day, I wanted to be prepared.

Detective Quinn agreed to the interview the second I called him to ask. Instead of being delighted by his change in attitude towards me, it was making me feel a little hopeless. No one thought I was going to make it through this trial. They were just pandering to me in the meantime. Of course, even while being helpful the detective had still managed to irritate me – because being a big giant pain in the rear was his default setting. Just before I hung up he said, 'You know, he's not going to talk to you. Gunnar, I mean. But if you want to waste your time, go for it.'

'He's probably right, you know,' Greg said, overhearing the latter part of the conversation. 'These Vlad's Boys don't talk. Ever. Y'know, unless it's to smear some vile graffiti about dayturners on every wall they find.'

'Well, that's why I want to be extra prepared,' I said, slamming the office phone back onto the receiver. 'I'm sure there's something among all this I can use to irritate Gunnar into talking.'

Greg grinned. 'That sounds like something Grace would say.'

'Hey.' I scooted closer to him and lowered my voice. 'Speaking of Grace, what's with all the fifties glam? I mean, don't get me wrong – her apartment looks almost as amazing as she does but … she's a witch, right? Not a vampire?'

'You're surprised she's a witch? You expected her to be a vampire because of how she dresses? So … what? You think vampires spend their lives stuck in some fashion time warp from the decade they were turned?' Greg almost spat out his coffee.

'Don't they? I mean, I'm still wearing the same outfits I wore in the early noughties. You find something you like, you stick with it. Well, if you're lazy like me you do, anyway. That's why I'm confused about Grace. I figured maybe a vamp would enjoy dressing the way they did in their heyday, but Grace is only forty or so, and she's a witch. So she couldn't have been around in the fifties. Could she?'

Greg popped a lollipop in his mouth and kept his eye on what he was doing. The guy seemed to have an endless supply of snacks. 'Vamps aren't the only ones who can live long lives. Witches can be pretty old, too. Some look younger because of glamour spells. Some stay physically young forever because of dark magic.'

I glanced up towards the apartment. 'So which is it with Grace?'

Greg kept sucking his lollipop, and shrugged. 'I've never met anyone who dared to ask her, so I've no idea.'

I wasn't so sure I'd be brave enough either, I thought, continuing to leaf through one of Greg's books. It was all about vampires, and their seemingly endless powers.

'They can move things with their mind?' I asked. 'For real?'

'Some can. Remember the pager I was waving around yesterday? Well, it wasn't a pager.'

'Oh gee, really?'

He gave me a sheepish smile. 'Yeah, I kind of figured you hadn't fallen for my brilliant ruse. Anyway, it was a telekinetic scanner. It basically lights up if there's been a lot of telekinetic activity in the area – like, if a vampire has been using their mental powers to do things we couldn't see them do with the naked eye. They can move really quickly, and vaporize themselves so we can't see them. They're super strong, and the older and more powerful among them can move things with the power of their mind. Oh, and a rare few can read minds, too. Like Pru and her family.'

Oh dear. I'd have to learn to think quietly while I was in the Vander Inn.

'And your scanner thingy was flashing green,' I said, forcing myself to stay on track. 'So that means there *was* a vampire doing some of that on the train. But … for what? So they could add the Night potion to Bathsheba's smoothie and get rid of the evidence without being detected?'

Greg nodded. 'That seems to be Dylan's working theory. But scanners will only tell you so much. Luckily, a scanner isn't the only tool I use. I've been developing some better tech. It's still experimental, but it allows me to see the actual patterns of the telekinetic activity.'

With an excitable look on his face, he popped a flash drive into the computer, and I found myself looking at photos of the train carriage – except they were *not* average photos. It was as if a coloured wave had been superimposed onto each picture.

He pointed to one of them. It was of the table closest to the door joining the dining carriage to the carriage behind. I could see a haze of red and green, leading from the table to the kitchen. He brought up two more photos, all with a similar colour pattern.

'This activity is what I caught through one of my camera filters after each murder. The colours you see are telekinetic activity. But there would have been no reason for the waiters on the train to use their vampire powers. People like service to move slowly on the Riddler's Express. The whole old-fashioned vibe it has going on is part of its charm.' He brought up a fourth photograph. 'And this is what my filters caught after Bathsheba's murder.'

He chewed on his lollipop stick, looking troubled. I could see why. There was a haze of red and green again, but this time there was a lot more red than green. The pattern was haphazard, drifting all over the carriage, much less organised than the previous murders.

I pulled up the detective's reports, checking quickly through them all. 'Hang on a minute,' I said. 'Gunnar wasn't even *on* duty for the first of those murders. But … then why do the first three look the same, and the last one is the one that looks different? If Gunnar was the one who killed Bathsheba, then surely it ought to be the other way around.'

'Yeah, I've been wondering the same myself. But there's something else you need to know about vampires, Ash. They can turn into a bat and fly. And when I say they can fly, I mean they can fly *really* fast. Gunnar could have murdered Bathsheba without anyone knowing he was on the train.

Flown in and out, then kept himself vaporized while he was on the train so no one would notice him. Or it could have been another member of Vlad's Boys. It doesn't change the fact that Gunnar is a member of a gang who have sworn to kill dayturners. Even if he didn't do *all* of the murders, he probably did this one, while someone else did the first three. Maybe this one was his first – the haywire telekinetic activity would be explained if it *was* his first. Nerves, inexperience … but Ash, whether Gunnar committed one of these murders, or all of them, he *is* one of Vlad's Boys. Dylan did right to arrest him. That gang is scum. One of them off the street is better than nothing.'

I sat back, looking at it all from a distance. Sometimes a less concentrated eye helped me pick out things, see patterns that I wouldn't have otherwise. But no matter what way I looked at it all, the patterns of activity were the same for every murder except Bathsheba's. And yeah, it *could* be explained by Gunnar being inexperienced. But I just wasn't sure.

We kept working together for the rest of the day, (albeit with plenty of breaks for snacks). Greg was so much fun to work with that I barely noticed the time passing.

'I didn't know what happened to the others, you know,' he told me as we packed up our things at the end of the day. 'Arnold told me to act evasive, not give anything away, see what they figured out for themselves. I had no idea he performed a memory spell when he let them go. I really don't want the same thing to happen to you.'

'What will be will be, I guess,' I said, doing my best to appear nonchalant. 'But on a positive note – you definitely handled the whole evasive thing well.'

He gave me a rueful smile. 'Yeah, sorry about that. Listen, I'm going to head off and get a good night's sleep for our little trip tomorrow. Can I give you a lift back to the Vander Inn?'

I shook my head. 'Thanks, but it's only a five minute walk. Hey, should I do anything else to prepare for this trip to Witchfield?'

He plucked a stick of liquorice from behind his ear. 'Maybe pick up some travel sickness pills,' he suggested as he began to chew.

14. Fish Fingers

Fuzz had disappeared halfway through the day, but as I was walking out of the office he met me by the door and leapt into my arms. 'I was going to go straight home,' I said to him. 'But it's just occurred to me that you've had quite a busy day – which means you're probably hungry?'

I felt him purr against my chest.

'Okay, so.' I patted his head. 'We'll take a little trip to the shop before we go home. See if there's anything there that takes your fancy. I could do with a bar of chocolate myself. A big one. Actually, a huge one.'

The shop was busy, as always. Now that I knew a little more about the supernatural world, the wide variety of vegan food for sale suddenly made sense. Almost all weredogs, apparently, were vegan. Greg told me it was because they ate out of bins for three nights every month, and preferred to be healthy the rest of the time. I was a little bit afraid to ask Edward, the Daily Riddler's only weredog employee, if that was true. Either way, I'd definitely seen Edward drink a lot of chocolate soymilk.

I put Fuzz under one arm and picked up a basket with the other. 'Now, I know I can't understand you,' I said in a low voice as we headed for the tinned fish. 'But if you could just let me know what you like to eat, it'd be great. Do you like tinned salmon?'

Fuzz shook his head.

'Tuna?'

He nodded enthusiastically, and I picked up a few tins, then grabbed some chocolate bars from another aisle before heading to the cash register.

Norman's mother, Norma, was there. She had a red glove on one hand, and was knitting another. 'What a lovely little cat,' she said.

Fuzz purred.

'I have six little girls myself. There's Princess Preciousbottom, Queen Swishytail, Lady Lightpaws, the Duchess of Riddler's Edge, the Dowager Queen, and the Lady in Waiting. What's this little fella called?'

'Fuzz.' Sure, it seemed less fancy than the names of Norma's cats, but at least it was his choice. But what did I know? Maybe Norma's cats liked their names.

Norma looked the cat in the eyes as she scanned my purchases. 'Well, Fuzz, the door to my little ladies' cat flap is closed to any cat who doesn't have a special collar. So if you want to court them, it has to be under my supervision.'

Judging by the way his purrs increased, I had the sense he would be taking that as a challenge.

≈

Pru and Nollaig had told me to treat the Vander Inn like a home from home. I didn't bother telling them that to do so would require me having an actual home in the first place, because really, who wanted to know about the barrenness of my tiny flat, a place that I'd never added so much as a cushion to?

For all its Victorian quirks, the Vander Inn already felt like more of a home than my Dublin rental, so I felt perfectly comfortable to head to the kitchen when I got back. I knew that Pru and her mother were asleep, so I did try to curb my usual clumsiness as I washed Fuzz's morning bowl and prepared him a fresh feed. He did his part too, bless him – if you call wrapping his way around my legs and almost tripping me up helping.

I was just throwing the empty tuna tin into the bin when a shadow fell over the room. The hair on my arms and on the back of my neck stood to attention, and my spine grew ramrod straight.

'You must be Arnold's latest,' a husky voice said in a London accent.

I turned to look at the person who had spoken. He was a little taller than me, with bleached blond hair and ice-blue eyes. He was wearing a tight white T-shirt and blue jeans, and had an amazing thin-but-toned body going on. As he crossed the kitchen and extended a hand, my head began to feel a little empty and fizzy, and my throat went dry.

'I … I have fish fingers,' I said, keeping my hand pasted firmly by my side. Fish fingers? Oh, Aisling, however have you managed to work as a wordsmith all these years?

He smiled, slow and broad, looking at my hands. 'They look like perfectly acceptable fingers to me.'

My throat was still dry, and I could feel that my cheeks were flaming red. His smile was even broader now, and he was shining those ice-blue eyes right into mine. A shiver worked its way down my spine, and he said, 'Cold? I can turn up the central heating.'

'I … no, I'm not cold. I … need to wash my hands. I was feeding Fuzz.'

He looked in interest at Fuzz, who was already halfway through his supper. 'Since when do we have a cat in the house? Cats hate us.'

'Us?' I rushed to the sink and concentrated very hard on scrubbing my hands. Maybe if I didn't look at him, I wouldn't feel so … so … so *what?* I thought about the guy on the train with the long hair who asked me to sit next to him. My supernatural swotting had told me he had to be a werewolf. Apparently, they had some pheromone thing going on that made them wildly attractive. But this guy said *us*. Did that make him a vampire? 'Are you a guest here?' I asked.

He moved right beside me, plucked an apple from a bowl and tossed it in the air before taking a bite. Oh, dear goddess, why was that so sexy? And what was with me saying *dear goddess*? Was I so easily influenced? And … did vampires even *eat* apples? Whatever this guy was, he was crunching into that fruit with gusto.

'I'm Jared,' he said between crunches. 'Nollaig's son.'

I turned off the tap and began to dry my hands. 'Nollaig's son? But you're London.' I slapped my forehead. 'Sorry, I mean … you have a London accent.'

He tossed his apple core into a bin and sat up on the counter. 'I do. I stayed with Dad when he and Mam ended things. I've spent the last two hundred years living in England. But I like to come visit whenever I can. Pru might be a fortune-telling weirdo, but she's the best sister a vampire could ask for.' He arched a brow. 'Hey, I don't need to go and compel you to forget this conversation, do I? When I phoned Pru this morning she told me you were up to speed on what we are.'

I felt my body stiffen, and noticed that Fuzz had the same reaction. The cat left his bowl, jumped up into my arms, and hissed at Jared. 'I'm up to speed,' I said coldly. 'But I'm a bit sick of people talking about messing about in my brain.'

Jared held his hands up. 'Sorry, I was just joking. A bad joke, obviously. But what do you mean about people messing about in your brain?'

I began to stroke Fuzz and took a seat at the kitchen table, holding him firmly in my arms. Unlike the tables in the dining room, it was devoid of doilies and cloths. The whole kitchen had a shabby chic vibe, and I felt incredibly comfortable there. Perhaps that was why I began to pour out pretty much everything that had happened, since the moment I went to lunch with Arnold.

Jared pulled out a chair and sat beside me (very close beside me – I guess he didn't have personal space issues) shaking his head in surprise and making shocked noises at all the right places. 'I can't believe it,' he said when I'd finished. He reached out and patted my hand. 'I knew that the old geezer was going through staff like the clappers, but I didn't know it was anything like that. For the love of Dracula!' He had just begun to stroke my hand in a firm but soft motion, when Pru entered the room.

'Hey!' She gave Jared a playful slap across the back of the head. 'Enough of that, you dirty old Lothario! Can't I have *one* friend you don't try it on with?'

He let out a throaty laugh, then stood up and pulled her into a hug. 'Missed you too, Sis. Hey, did you know about all this? Arnold Albright wiping reporters' memories if they don't get the job?'

Pru sighed and moved away from him, slumping down into a chair. 'I only found out recently.'

'We should report him to the Wayfairs. You're only supposed to wipe humans' memories in extreme situations. I don't think this quite counts.'

'It's the Wayfarers now, actually.' Pru rolled her eyes. 'But I can see why you'd fail to have kept up with that incredibly important political development. I mean, what with all the rich ladies you have to entertain.'

I felt my face flush. What was he? Some sort of gigolo?

'You'll make Ash think I'm some sort of gigolo!' he cried. He looked at me, and I did my best not to squirm. 'I'm not, I swear. I run an art gallery in London. Some of my buyers just happen to be rich women. I can't help it if they want to spend a million quid on a picture of a toilet.'

Pru stood up and moved to the cooker. There was a huge pot on top, and she turned the ring on and began to heat it up. 'Mam made a stew,' she said. 'Oh, and speaking of Mam.' She turned to her brother. 'I *know* she didn't know you're coming, because she would have told me. Whose husband have you annoyed this time?'

Jared cleared his throat. 'I think that's my cue to leave.' He bowed deeply, then grabbed my hand and kissed it. It was all I could do not to fan my face. 'It was a pleasure to meet you, Ash. I'll be sticking around for quite a while, so I hope we get to know each other a *lot* better.'

As soon as he left the room I placed Fuzz back at his bowl and rushed over to Pru. She was stirring the stew, and it smelled delicious. 'Em … I have a question. Do vampires have the same pheromone thing going on as werewolves?'

She shook her head. 'Not quite. We're supposedly super attractive, but I don't see it myself. But for some reason, humans get a bit lusty around us. Weird if you ask me. Why? You don't fancy my brother, do you? Because I have to tell you, he's a bit of a ladies' man.'

I bit my lip. I didn't fancy him, did I? I mean, sure, he was devastatingly attractive. And there was that accent, and that way he had of moving. Sort of cat-like, but not cat-like in the sneaky way that John, my editor, had of moving. Jared's movement was lithe, dangerous and sensual.

But he was *not* my type. The hair was all wrong. He was tall, but not tall enough. And he clearly loved himself, a trait that always turned me cold. I liked my men to be a little more humble. With darker eyes. And maybe a lighthouse. Okay, I realise what I've just said, but Detective Quinn is the exception to that. He might have just about every trait I find attractive in a man, but I did *not* find him attractive. Not one little bit. Jared, on the other hand … he had none of the qualities I usually went for. And yet …

'Nah.' I shook my head. 'I was just wondering. Because of what you said about him being a Lothario.'

'Uh huh.' She gave me a knowing smile. 'Well, if you ever happen to change your mind, please feel free to *not* give me the details. But I've got to say, I was sure you had a thing for our handsome local detective.'

Was I *that* obvious? My eyes widened, but I did my best to rein in my surprise. 'I have no idea what you're talking about,' I told her. 'And if you've come to that conclusion because you've been reading my mind, then you've clearly been reading the wrong thoughts.'

That same knowing smile was still on her pretty face. If I didn't like her so much, I'd hate her. 'Anyway,' I went on, 'he's taken, isn't he? I mean, there are all those photos of the supermodel in his house.'

'The supermodel?' Pru scrunched up her nose as she went to the fridge. She pulled out a bottle of wine. 'Oh, you must mean Darina Berry. Yeah, they were a big deal for a while. They were engaged to be married, but she left him a while back. Oh, and speaking of our dashing detective …' She paused while she grabbed two glasses and filled them with Pinot Grigio. 'Maybe don't tell him my brother is back.'

'Oh?' I took a sip of the wine. 'Why's that?'

Pru's face turned troubled. 'They just have a bit of a hate-on for each other. I have no idea why. But trust me – if they cross paths, it's not going to be pretty.'

≈

I woke up with Fuzz curled up into the crook of my arm, after yet another amazing night's sleep. Of course, last night it might have had less to do with the glorious bed and more to do with the glorious wine.

Jared had brought a couple of cases with him, and we enjoyed some over dinner, and some after dinner, too. Sure, there were one or two moments during the evening when I noticed something *other* than wine in my hosts' glasses, but hey ho. Nollaig had been out for the night, so Pru, Jared and I enjoyed a vampire movie marathon. They pointed out the inconsistencies, and I just sat back and drank in the atmosphere as much as the wine.

I'd never been with any of my foster-brothers and -sisters long enough to develop a bond. Despite all their bickering, that was exactly what Pru and Jared had together – a deep, heartfelt bond. The evening with them was one of the most enjoyable I'd had in a long time, and by the time I went up to bed, I was feeling completely at home. But just as I'd been climbing into my comfiest pyjamas, I noticed an unread text message. It was from Arnold Albright:

Grace has updated me on the situation. I'm sorry you had to find out like that, and I feel the need to explain things further. If you're not too annoyed with me, I'd love it if you would join me for dinner in the Fisherman's Friend at seven, tomorrow night.

I texted back a quick response. Yeah, I was definitely going to join the old goat for dinner. But I wasn't going to let him off easy. Come Friday, I'd most likely be leaving Riddler's Edge forever. Perhaps Arnold's memory mojo wouldn't be such a bad thing, after all – at least I wouldn't be able to remember how much I liked it here.

15. Wizardly Wagon

I stood in front of the Vander Inn, waiting for Greg and enjoying the smell of the sea air. I could see the harbour off in the distance, and hear the sounds of the fishermen going about their morning.

'You look pretty fresh for a woman who stayed up so late.'

I jumped at the sound of Jared's voice. 'Shouldn't you be in bed?' I asked as I turned around.

He gave me a wicked smile. 'It felt a bit big and lonely in my bed, so I thought I'd get up and see you off. Here, I made you this.' He handed me a flask and a lunchbox. 'I noticed you didn't eat any breakfast.'

I felt my face begin to flush. He had actually made me a packed lunch? Only my astronomy obsessed foster-mother had ever done that. 'Thanks,' I said. 'That was really nice of you.'

He seemed like he was just about to reply, when his eyes narrowed. He was looking out onto the road, as Detective Quinn's car drove by. I looked into the driver's seat, and the detective was looking Jared's way, a full-on scowl on his face. As soon as he was out of sight, Jared's demeanour relaxed.

'As much as I hope you enjoy your lunch,' he said. 'I hope you'll enjoy your dinner more. Because I was hoping that you'd agree to have dinner with me. There's a new restaurant in Riddler's Cove that I'd love to try out. The receptionist from the Daily Riddler owns it. So how about it? You me, and a stupidly expensive bottle of champagne.'

This guy was smooth, I'd give him that. So smooth that my knees were feeling a little jelly-like. And I really *did* want to check out Malachy's restaurant. Nevertheless, I was almost relieved that I had an excuse. 'I can't,' I said. 'I'm having dinner with Arnold.'

His expression darkened. 'So he can make excuses for the way he's been treating his reporters, no doubt.'

'Probably.' I shrugged. 'But I'm going along anyway.'

Jared let out a sigh. 'Of course you are. Because you're a decent person who's always willing to give someone a second chance. But just be on your guard, Ash. Most of the Albrights are lovely. I'd count them among the more pleasant witch covens. But Arnold … well, he didn't get to be one of the richest media moguls in the supernatural world by playing nice. Oh look – here's Greg now.'

I glanced out onto the road, where Greg's purple van was making its way towards us. He pulled up at the kerb and grinned. 'Hey Ash. Hey Jared – I didn't know you were back in town. Good to see you, mate.'

Jared grinned back at Greg. 'Good to see you, too. Hey, Ash has just turned me down for a date tonight. Fancy a boys' night on the town?'

'Definitely,' said Greg as I opened the door and climbed in next to him. 'I'll give you a text when I'm done at work.'

≈

'Welcome to Wizardly Wagon,' said Greg with a smile as I closed the door behind me.

'You call your van Wizardly Wagon? I always thought I'd name a car, if I had one long enough. I have a bit of a tendency to crash the poor things before we've had the chance to bond. Hey, you and Jared seem to be mates. Don't suppose you'd like to tell me why there's a problem between him and Detective Quinn?'

'I have no idea,' he said, far too quickly, before pulling two packets of peanuts from his pocket and passing one to me.

I loved peanuts, but I couldn't eat many unless I had a drink to wash them down, so I opened the flask. It was filled with black coffee that smelled like it had been brewed in heaven. 'You know, it wouldn't really matter if you did tell me.' I was speaking in my most casual tone as I poured some coffee out. 'You might as well go ahead and spill, seeing as I'll have forgotten it all by the weekend.'

Greg snorted. 'Sure – and why don't I tell you all my deepest and darkest secrets while we're at it?'

'Well, I'm all ears. Although I have to say, you don't seem like the sort of guy who has deep, dark secrets.'

'I wish that were true.' He frowned. 'Anyway, did you read the notes I gave you about Witchfield?'

I sipped my coffee. It didn't just smell like heaven. It tasted like it, too. 'Yeah, I looked over it,' I replied. I did *not* add that I'd forgotten all about it until I was in the bath this morning. It was completely unlike me to forget to study up on anything. I was the queen of nerds. But spending time with Jared and Pru had thrust it clean from my mind.

Luckily, I read fast, and thanks to Greg's notes I now knew that Witchfield was the largest supernatural prison in the world. I also knew that its position constantly shifted, so getting there required following a changeable set of magical coordinates. 'I'm kind of confused about how we're going to get there,' I admitted. 'Witches travel by flying on brooms or clicking their fingers, and it seems like it only exists in some witchy region so … how are a wizard and a human going to get to it?'

He grinned. 'I'm glad you asked that. Witches aren't the only ones who can use brooms to travel. Wizards have brooms of their own, too. Better than witch brooms, in fact. The broom itself is *way* more magical than a witch broom, so you don't need power to ride it.'

I gulped. 'We're … we're flying a *broom* to the prison?'

There was a look on Greg's face that reminded me of a kid at Christmas. He was practically thrumming with excitement. 'Kind of,' he said. 'Except that you're already in it. It's an experimental design, though, so prepare for a *lot* of lurching.'

I gawped at him. 'Your van? Is a broom?'

'In a way. I modified the tech that wizards use to make brooms, and installed it in my van. Did you take the travel sickness pills?'

I shook my head, groaning. 'I forgot to buy any. Hey, when you say *experimental design* what do you mean, exactly? Have you tested this yet?'

He cleared his throat before replying. 'I have every reason to believe that this journey will be a success. Maybe you'd better put on your seatbelt, though. Just to be on the safe side.'

≈

About ten minutes later, we arrived in front of the gates of Witchfield Prison. It had been the longest ten minutes of my life, and I was sincerely glad that I hadn't got much more in my stomach than a handful of peanuts and a cup of coffee.

First, he had keyed half a dozen sets of coordinates into a keypad on his van's dash. Next, he had pressed a series of brightly coloured buttons. After that, I was too ill to follow a thing he did.

It's difficult to explain what it feels like to be in a flying van, but I think I can cut to the crux by simply saying that I wouldn't recommend it. Once we were in the air, the landscape below began to continually shift, coinciding with a series of sickening lurches and flashes of light.

My hair was a mess. My stomach was heaving. But I had gotten there, in one dishevelled piece.

'Wow.' Greg shook his head in amazement. 'I did *not* think that was going to work. Well? You ready?'

I shot him the sort of look I usually reserved for door-to-door salespeople, and climbed out of the van.

16. Rat in a Cage

No matter how much Greg had told me, and no matter how much I had read, there was nothing in the world that could have prepared me for Witchfield. The building itself was unfathomably big, with walls that definitely weren't hewn from average stone. The exact building material wasn't generally disclosed, because avoiding mass break-outs is always an advantage in a prison.

The guards were all dressed like Gretel had been, and they placed cuffs around my wrists even though I had as much magic as a gnat. Greg didn't get the shackle treatment, but he did get just about every gadget he had inspected, and one or two things were taken from him.

'But I need that, Walter.' Greg was pleading with a burly guard and pointing to a sparkly purple wand. 'It's an OAP!'

I resisted the urge to laugh. My research had told me that an OAP was an acronym for an object of awesome power. But just because I knew what it meant didn't make it any less hysterical.

'You'll get it back on the way out,' Walter said impassively. 'You're lucky I'm letting you keep anything. You know, your tech is about a million times ahead of anything *we* have. You ever think of selling any of it to us?'

Greg gave the guard a tight smile. 'Never in a million years. And if I find out anyone's been fiddling with my wand while I'm inside …'

Walter laughed, and waved us through.

The prison was split into wings, because there were different requirements needed to suppress the different kinds of power. Greg had assured me that not a single vampire in Gunnar's wing would be able to read our minds or use their power in any way. I guess I'd just have to take his word on that one.

We were led straight to Gunnar's cell, and a couple of seats had been set up outside for us. I say cell, but the bars weren't exactly what you'd call solid. I could barely see them at all, other than the usual kaleidoscope haze that let me know when magic was at work. Either way, we could see and hear Gunnar through the bars, and he could see and hear us.

'Hello, Gunnar,' I said brightly. 'How's prison life treating you?'

He glared at me. 'Is that some sort of joke? What in Dracula's name are you doing here, anyway? You're a human. I can smell your stink a mile away.'

'Hey! I used a very nice lime-scented soap this morning, I'll have you know. Anyway, we're not here to talk about how delightful I smell. We're here to interview you for the paper. We're doing a special piece in Friday's evening edition, and we'd like to get your point of view on the matter. We'd like to know why you have a particular dislike for dayturners, why you're such a surly waiter … that sort of thing.'

Gunnar looked away from me and spat on the floor. Lovely. The dishwater-grey prison uniform didn't have a very high collar, and I could see his tattoo more clearly than ever. 'It's a bit weird, isn't it? That tattoo of yours. I mean, if *I* was about to commit a bunch of murders, I'd probably try and be less obvious about it. But here you are, wearing your Vlad's Boys affiliation loud and proud.'

He spat again. Greg was messing about with filters, taking photos while I talked. I doubted many people would enjoy seeing a picture of a spitting murderer, so I had to assume he was doing something wizardly.

'Another thing I find interesting,' I went on, 'is the fact that you were only on duty for three of the recent murders. I guess that means you're a lot more talented at the whole vampire thing than you look, or else … or else there's someone else involved. Another member of Vlad's Boys, maybe? One who isn't dumb enough to wear a tattoo?'

He was still looking away from me, but his fists were clenched with agitation, so I pressed on. 'I bet Detective Quinn's already offered you a deal. I mean, that's the kind of thing I'd do if I were in charge of the investigation. See if I could get you a couple of years off your sentence in return for info on the other killer. Or killers. Maybe even a whole *heap* of years off for information on who's actually running Vlad's Boys. Because that's a big secret, or so I'm told.'

His undead eyes flashed towards me. 'And it's going to stay that way, human.' He sat forward on his bed. It looked narrow and uncomfortable, but he hardly deserved a thick mattress and a king-sized bed. 'I might be in a cage right now, but that doesn't make me a rat. I admire the people I work with. I'd go so far as to say I even care for one or two of them. And I do *not* rat out my people. I know all about the human world. I know that loyalty is just a word your leaders use to suppress the masses. But vampires, vampires know the true meaning of loyalty. It's just one of the reasons why we're the superior species.'

'Species?' I glanced down at my notes. 'You think you're a species? You're not a species, Gunnar. Vampirism is a virus. A virus that's constantly changing. And you know what I think? I think no one actually knows why the dayturner strain came about. I think that you could wake up tomorrow, and be the very thing you hate.'

His jaw started to saw, and he stood up and punched the air. 'Get out!' he cried, his teeth elongating into *very* sharp points. 'Get out before I show you what a vampire *really* is.'

I stood up, placing an even smile on my face. 'I think we have quite enough for the article,' I told Greg. 'Are you happy with the pictures you've taken?'

'Very,' he said, slinging his camera around his neck. 'Let's go and get a nice lunch, shall we?'

'Somewhere fancy,' I added. 'And outdoors. I do like to be able to sit outside and enjoy the fresh air while I eat.'

17. The Best Man for the Job

Well, I *was* enjoying the fresh air, if you count rolling down the window of Greg's van while we sat in the train station carpark. The journey back from Witchfield had been just as sickening as the journey there, and if my lunch hadn't been so darned delicious, I doubt I would have been able to stomach it.

'I'll check out the filters while we eat,' Greg said through mouthfuls of one of my sandwiches. There had been four in the lunchbox, so I decided it would be selfish not to share.

The sandwiches were stuffed with fresh tuna, sundried tomatoes and a whole lot of yumminess. There was even dessert, some sort of apple crumble with cream.

'How did he whip all this up this morning?' I wondered. 'And more importantly, how did he manage to fit it all into such a small lunchbox?'

Greg grinned, the gap between his teeth filled with something green. 'Jared's always been an amazing chef. And the lunchbox is bigger on the inside. Wizard tech.'

I shook my head in amazement as Greg leaned over and pressed on the bottom of the lunchbox, making a second, far larger layer appear. It was even bigger than the first, and it was filled with fresh-baked chocolate chip cookies. 'I wish I was a wizard. Hey, I haven't asked Pru this in case it's rude, but … I always thought vampires just consumed blood. And that they only went out at night.'

Greg wiped his hand and hooked his camera up to his laptop. 'They've evolved to be able to stand daylight over the years, but they much prefer the dark, and some vamps say their eyes sting during the day if they don't wear sunglasses. And as for blood, they need it to survive. But they like everyday food, same as the rest of us. There's a rumour the Vlad's Boys gang only drink blood. No other food or drink. But I doubt it's true.' He began to type quickly, somehow managing to steal three of my cookies at the same time. 'So, I wasn't taking normal photos of Gunnar, but I guess you figured that out. Grace would rather wear a pair of jeans than run a photo of one of Vlad's Boys. She has this idea that criminals get off on the exposure.'

'I agree with her,' I said, managing to snatch the last cookie for myself. 'So what were you doing? All of Gunnar's abilities are subdued while he's in Witchfield. What could your filters possibly pick up?'

He slurped some coffee. 'You know the way Grace was trying to see your power through her Aurameter? Well, I had this theory that *all* supernaturals have a unique aura around us. And it turned out, I was right. I've managed to fine-tune my software so that I can read auras as clearly as I can read fingerprints.' He pointed to the screen, where a photo of Gunnar in his cell had loaded. 'See that hue around him? How it's all orange and brown and scary looking? My first few trials only picked up things like that. Standard vamp aura. Not super-evil, just your run-of-the mill stupid young vampire. *But.*' He began to type in some commands, and the colours around Gunnar intensified. On the right side of the screen, some sort of script was running. It seemed to be listing out the strength of each colour in the aura.

'So you think that by refining it this much, you can identify a unique aura for every supernatural?'

'Exactly. And I've found a way to sync it up with crime-scene photos, too. Every recording of telekinetic activity has a unique signature. It's just been impossible to narrow down. Until now.' He opened up the photos he'd taken in the aftermath of Bathsheba's murder, and did some more frantic typing. Within a few seconds, a banner stretched across the screen: *Zero Percent Match.*

Greg paled. ‘Either my program isn’t worth the hundreds of hours I’ve spent writing it, or else … or else Gunnar used *no* telekinetic power whatsoever on the day Bathsheba was murdered. All of that telekinetic energy my filters picked up … it belongs to someone else entirely.’

‘And if Gunnar didn’t use any of his vampire powers,’ I said, my mind running a mile a minute, ‘then how on earth did he get rid of the evidence?’

≈

As the train pulled into the station after its latest Dublin to Riddler’s Edge run, Greg and I stood waiting for the driver. He got off, a wide smile on his face, wiping the sweat from his brow with a red neckerchief. I almost squealed right then. Not only did he have a red neckerchief, but he was also carrying a shovel, and he had coal stains on his hands.

‘It runs on coal!’ I gasped.

The train driver grinned. ‘Of a sort. I only have to add one shovel at the start of every journey. Good thing too, or I wouldn’t be able to manage it on my own.’ He tipped his cap. ‘I take it you’re the new reporter, seeing as you’re here with our Greg. What can I do for you both?’

I was too busy taking in the train driver, so Greg spoke. ‘Ash is writing an article for Friday’s evening edition,’ he said. ‘It’s going to be quite a comprehensive piece on the murder investigation so far.'

'Yeah, I am.' I finally stopped staring and found my voice. 'And I was wondering about the staff on the train. Who does the hiring? Because I find it a bit odd that *anyone* would employ a waiter with a Vlad's Boys tattoo to serve dayturners.'

The driver sighed and put his cap back on his head. 'As do I. And believe me, I've had words. But I have no say in hiring or firing. You'll have to speak to human resources about that. Mick Plimpton – he's your man.'

≈

The fact that a supernatural train service had a human resource manager was, honestly, the most surprising thing I'd learned since arriving in Riddler's Edge. Mick Plimpton's office was based in Dublin, in a witch enclave called Warren Lane. Just one of the many place names I had listed in my special notebook. Take that, John!

I would have been a lot more excited to see the place if it hadn't been for the fact that we were, once again, travelling in Greg's Wizardly Wagon. By the time we were parked on the street in Warren Lane, I was feeling so unwell that I couldn't even get giddy about the fact that a man was flying past me on a broom.

The office itself wouldn't have made *anyone* giddy, though. It was bland and modern, with a bland and modern man sitting behind a bland and modern desk, pretending to be too busy typing to speak to us. Eventually he looked up and said, 'Sorry, just had to shoot off a super-important email. What can I do you for?'

I shrugged. 'I've been accused of loitering in the past.'

His smile fell. 'It was a play on words.'

'And a hilarious one, too.' I sat forward. 'We're from the Daily Riddler. We were told you're in charge of hiring the staff on the Riddler's Express.'

A self-important look crossed his face. 'That's me. Mick Plimpton, human resources manager. Our little joke, of course. I'd never *actually* hire a human for one of our trains. Ugh! Whenever new staff is needed, Mick's your man! I have the final say on *every* staffing issue in the Irish supernatural train services. And I think I say with confidence that I am the *best* man for the job.'

'Oh?' I arched a brow. 'Well then you'll be just the man to tell me – how the hell did you think it was a good idea to hire someone from a well-known hate group? Did you actually think it was appropriate for Gunnar to serve meals to the very people his organisation has sworn to kill?'

His eyes darted to Greg. 'I … she … I've already spoken to Dylan Quinn about this. Why is this woman here, Greg?'

Greg fished a liquorice stick from one of his pockets and chewed it thoughtfully. 'You should address any questions you have to Ash. She's the boss.'

I smiled at Greg. 'I prefer to think of us as partners. But you're right. This *is* my story, so I'm not sure why Mr Plimpton here is ignoring me. Mr Plimpton?'

His lip curled. 'I didn't *know* Gunnar was a member of Vlad's Boys. I've only just heard about the tattoo, and trust me – he didn't have it when I interviewed him. We have many vampires working in our train services. The early and late routes seem to suit them. Why, on that route alone we have Suzette, Vikram and Miriam. Each and every one of them is an exemplary employee, and I find your line of questioning to be – quite frankly – racist against vampires.'

Greg looked like he was about to choke on his liquorice. I patted his back and glared at Mr Plimpton. 'If you're trying to shift the spotlight, Mr Plimpton, then you're failing miserably. I take no issue with your hiring vampires. I take issue with your hiring a member of Vlad's Boys. I came here today to get your take on that, and to make sure I accurately represented your point of view in my article.' I stood up. 'But I think I already have all I need.'

18. The Fisherman's Friend

When Greg and I returned to the office, he had to run off and help Grace with a computer emergency, so I typed up my notes alone, replaying the day's events in my mind. There was something that everyone was overlooking, I just knew there was. And seeing as this was the first story of mine that wouldn't have the juicy bits edited to death, I wanted to do it justice.

I read the report that Detective Quinn had submitted that morning, to see how his interview with Gunnar had gone. There wasn't much to read, though, because Gunnar had been just as unwilling to talk with the detective as he'd been with me.

With nothing new to read in the detective's latest report, I reread everything he had submitted previously, in case there was anything I missed. I wanted to check, in particular, if Mick Plimpton had been telling the truth about Gunnar's tattoo. But it seemed that it *was* a recent addition, just as he'd said. Detective Quinn wrote that he saw the tattoo for the first time on the day of Bathsheba's murder, even though he'd interviewed Gunnar before. And in those previous interviews, Gunnar had seemed like little more than your average jerk.

Every passenger and member of staff on the train had received thorough background checks, and I took another look through all of those, too. Some staff members seemed to have received a greater going over than others – the younger guys, in particular, because intelligence seemed to suggest that Vlad's Boys specifically recruited younger men.

Now that his tattoo made his affiliation so clear, it really did seem that Gunnar was the most likely suspect. If only it weren't for the pesky little matter of Greg's aura-reading equipment. I wondered how the detective would react when Greg and I offered him that evidence tomorrow. Probably with only slightly more crankiness than usual.

I was holding a well-chewed pen in one hand, my other hand poised at the computer keyboard, when a shadow fell across my desk.

'Still here?' asked Grace. She was holding a compact open, applying a fresh coat of lipstick.

'I was hoping to go over some things with Greg before the end of the day,' I said.

Grace laughed lightly. 'The end of the day has long passed. Greg's left the building. I saw him call out a goodbye to you, but you didn't seem to notice. You and I are the only ones left. And …' She glanced at her watch. '… you're almost late for your dinner with Arnold. Although I can't say I blame you if you want to take a rain check.'

I snatched up my purse and stood up. 'Good goddess, I didn't realise the time. I … I guess I'll see you tomorrow, then? I mean, unless Arnold's decided to bring the trial to an early end.' As I said it aloud, I realised that I was actually worried about that very thing. What if I came out of the Fisherman's Friend remembering nothing?

'He wouldn't dare end the trial early,' said Grace. She sat on the desk, giving me an even better look at her outfit. It was magnificent. A poodle skirt, red heels and a boat-neck sweater. 'Listen Aisling, I … well, Greg's been updating me on your progress. And I just want to say, it sounds like you're doing an adequate job.' She stood up once more and snapped her compact shut. 'Enjoy your dinner. It's not a supernatural establishment, but it's an interesting little place if you're in the mood for that sort of thing. Oh, but whatever you do, do not order the seafood platter.' She clicked her fingers, and disappeared.

For a moment I stood there, gaping at the spot where she'd just been. Sure, I'd read all about the whole finger-clicking thing, but boy oh boy! There had been many moments in life when I'd wished I could click my fingers and disappear. Tonight's dinner might just end with such a moment. But seeing as I didn't have magic at my fingertips, I picked up my bag and walked to the door.

≈

Now that I was standing out in front of the Fisherman's Friend, it didn't look olde-worlde – it just looked ancient. Like the tavern I'd been to in Riddler's Cove, it too had a thatched roof. But *this* thatch clearly needed work. It was thinning in spots, and nearly non-existent in others. The stonework of the building was higgledy-piggledy, and to be honest, I wasn't sure how it remained standing.

I pushed the door open gingerly, afraid that it would fall off its hinges, and entered a dark room. I had to step down into it, and even then the ceiling beams felt too close for comfort. I wondered what someone as tall as Detective Quinn or even Greg would do in a place like this. Probably stoop.

I could see Arnold in a booth in the far corner, waving at me. As I went to walk over, I noticed he wasn't the only person I knew. Greg, Pru and Jared were seated at the bar, drinking stout and eating steak and chips.

'I'll be with you in a sec,' I called to Arnold, and made my way to the bar. 'I know you said you were having a boys' night out,' I said. 'But this place wasn't quite what I imagined. And also, I'm pretty sure Pru is a girl.'

Pru tossed back some stout, burped, and then smiled at me. 'I'm an honorary bloke tonight, and I intend to act like one.'

'Of course,' I said. 'And what about the two of you?' I arched a brow at Greg and Jared. 'This is your usual haunt when you're out for the night?'

Jared gave an oh-so-innocent shrug. 'It could be. I'm quite enjoying the local colour.'

I glanced around the pub. There were three old men sitting at one end of the bar, and an even older two seated on stools by the fireplace. They all wore heavy black coats and caps, and not a single one of them was talking.

'Uh huh. Local colour.' Seeing as Greg was staying silent, I turned to him. 'And that's your answer, too? You're also here for the local colour?'

Greg's face reddened. 'I ... well ... y'know ...'

'Eloquently put. Well, I have to get over to Arnold. See you guys around.'

As I turned to walk away, Pru caught me by the hand and said, 'Wait. We're here because of you, okay? We just want to make sure Arnold doesn't do anything funny.'

Greg looked down into his pint. 'We want you to get the job, Ash. I'm getting sick of reporters coming and going. Pru really likes you. I like working with you. And, well, Jared just likes you because you're so pretty. So will you do us a favour and come and chat with us when you're done? So we can make sure you're still … intact?'

Aw! I was coming over all warm and fuzzy. Sure, Jared probably *did* just care because I was the latest female in town. But Pru and Greg really were two of the nicest people I'd ever met. Okay, so Greg was *also* the nuttiest, and the one with the most snacks on his person at any given time. But you could be nutty *and* nice, and Greg was the living proof.

'But if I've lost my memory, how will I remember to come and talk to you guys?'

'Good point,' Jared said. 'If you don't come to us, we'll come to you. And we'll be keeping an eye out the whole time, okay? If you need us, just holler.'

'Thanks guys.' I felt a genuine swell of fondness, and had to stop myself from hugging the three of them. 'I'll see you later.'

I joined Arnold in his booth, sliding in across from him. The fabric on the seats was a little on the shabby side, but it sure was comfortable.

'I see you're making friends.' Arnold nodded in the direction of the bar.

I picked up a menu and began to study it. 'Mm hm,' I said quietly. The menu was far shorter than the one on the train. There was steak and chips, lamb stew, and a seafood platter. There was a choice of apple tart with ice cream or apple tart with custard for dessert.

Arnold seemed about to say something when a waitress approached. She was a woman in her sixties or so, with dyed red hair and the sort of outfit that made her look like a medieval wench. 'Welcome to the Fisherman's Friend,' she said. 'I'm Bod's wife, Biddy.' She pointed to the bar, where a man with an eye-patch and a fake parrot on his shoulder was pouring a pint. How had I missed *him* when I walked in? 'That's Bod,' said Biddy. 'Now, I know Arnold very well, but I've never seen you before, my love.'

I pasted a smile on my face. 'Well, you probably won't be seeing much of me in the future, either. Arnold has me on trial at the Daily Riddler, and he's *very* fussy about who he hires.'

'The Daily Riddler!' Biddy's blue eyes widened, and a crazed look took over her face. 'I just love their puzzles. Will you be adding more? Please say you'll be adding more.'

'That's not really my department,' I said. 'I'm covering local news and events.'

'Oh.' Biddy's face fell. 'Well, that's almost as good as doing the puzzles, I suppose. Although not much happens here. The local choir will be singing sea shanties in a fortnight. That might be worth covering. So what can I get you? The seafood platter's on special offer. A platter for two is only a fiver. We'll even throw in free chips.'

'Thanks, but I can't stand seafood.' Actually, I loved seafood almost as much as I loved minestrone soup. But if you could get a platter for five quid, then it was probably best to heed Grace's warning. 'I'll have the steak and chips.'

'Me too,' said Arnold. 'And we'll have a bottle of your finest red.'

Biddy scribbled our orders down quickly, and went to walk away. 'I'll have a lemonade, actually,' I called after her. 'Not much of a wine drinker.' Another lie. But I wasn't about to drink anything Arnold gave me tonight. I'd be watching my lemonade like a hawk, too, because as soon as I looked away, he'd probably slip a potion into my glass.

'You're suspicious of me,' he said sadly. 'I can't say I blame you. By now you know that I lied about my daughter. Her position has been vacant for far longer than I led you to believe. And though I wish she were, she isn't spending her time writing crime novels.' He let out a long sigh. 'Dylan *never* should have told you the things he did. He's made it all so much more difficult for you. I might have to have a word with his superiors, see if I can get him moved from Riddler's Edge.'

For about ten seconds, I just stared. He still had that sweet old man expression on his face, all benign and innocent. But he was so far from innocent in all of this. 'You ...' I began, shaking my head. 'You …' I continued, clearly getting into my stride. 'You can't …'

Biddy arrived with our drinks, and I clutched my lemonade while I waited for her to leave.

'This is *not* Detective Quinn's fault!' I hissed once she was out of earshot. 'I pestered him into telling me the truth, and I still don't think he would have told me a thing if he hadn't thought I could handle it. He is a *good* man. A cantankerous one, maybe, but a good one, and if you try and get him relocated you'll probably make an enemy of pretty much everyone in Riddler's Edge. And what does it matter, anyway? He could have told me the biggest secret in the world, and it wouldn't matter a jot. You're just going to go and wipe my memory on Friday, the way you did with the other reporters. So why shouldn't I know the truth, even if it's just for a little while? And–' Once again, I had to pause while Biddy arrived. This time she had our meals, and she chatted for at least two minutes before leaving the table.

By the time she was gone, I was all out of anger. I just stared at Arnold, shaking my head. 'You know what? It doesn't matter. You'll just go ahead and do what you want. Just tell me though, will you – what *is* the criteria that a person has to meet in order *not* to get their memory wiped?'

He had begun to cut into his steak, and he ate about a quarter of it before answering. 'You've already surpassed the others. Grace tells me that

Dylan believes you can see things. He told her, apparently, that you could see the Wandering Wood. He said that you were figuring it all out on your own, anyway, and that all he did was help things along. I do believe you might just be the person I'm looking for. I have every confidence that you'll pass the final trial on Friday.'

I sat back, arms folded, regarding him. Sure, I hadn't eaten since lunch time, but the thought of eating with him was suddenly turning my stomach. He still had that sweet-guy smile on his face, like he thought he was doing me a favour by giving me this opportunity in the first place. 'You're not just looking for any old reporter, are you? You're looking for something more than that. I mean, there are people all over Ireland who know about the supernatural world and who help you keep it quiet. Like John. I'll bet his whole job is to make sure the real stories never make it as far as the public.'

His smile widened, and he put down his cutlery and clapped his hands. 'You really *are* the best candidate, by far. I knew it as soon as I met you.'

I sniffed my lemonade, and took a cautious sip. 'You should record your conversations, you know. I think that listening back to them might give you some valuable insight into your many personality flaws. I've seen the Daily Riddler's employment records, and every single one of those reporters whose memory you wiped would have been an excellent candidate for *any* newspaper. Each of them deserved the job on journalistic merit alone. So just come out and tell me, what are you really looking for? You might as well. I'll have forgotten it come Friday.'

He drained a full glass of wine before replying. Once he set the glass back on the table, I could see that the false smile had finally left his face. But it wasn't replaced by the wiliness I expected to see in its place. Instead, he looked sad. Deeply, truly sad. 'All right,' he said. 'I'll tell you. I *am* looking for someone in particular. I'm looking for my granddaughter.'

19. Family Ties

'Once there was a little girl,' said Arnold, refilling his glass and sitting back. 'And she was the loveliest little girl in the world. Her hair was a golden shade of red, her eyes were as blue as the sky, and her father loved her more than anything. Her mother had died in childbirth, so it was just the two of them, and yet it never felt lonely. They were so alike, you see. Kindred spirits. She loved to read and write, just as her father did. And oh, the stories she concocted.'

He paused to wipe a tear from his eye, and I waited patiently, not wanting to say a thing that might make him stop.

'As she grew older, she grew headstrong. But her father didn't mind, not at first. She was a chip off the old block, as they say. She started to work for one of his newspapers, and her stubbornness ensured she *always* uncovered the real story. Her articles won awards all over the supernatural world. Her father couldn't have been prouder. But then … then another man entered her life. She and her father fought about it, and she refused to leave this man. He was all wrong for her, she just couldn't see it. But her father could. And he thought that, with a good dose of tough love, she would see it too.' His voice trailed off, and he gazed down into his wine glass. He had long forgotten about the remainder of his steak, and all of his chips were as cold and uneaten as mine.

For a few minutes I remained patient, but when he said nothing more, I finally spoke. 'Arnold, you have to tell me the rest. What do you mean tough love? What did you do? Did you find a way to break them up?'

He tossed back his wine and gasped. 'Oh, I did more than that. I found a spell that would break the bond this young man had with my daughter. And I … I ensured that my daughter would never find him again, not even if she searched until the end of time.' He took another drink and gasped again. 'I tried to make her forget him, too. I tried a spell that would bond her to me, and make sure she never left me. I … I loved her, you see. And she was only going to choose the wrong sort of man again. I knew that I could make a better choice for her, when it was time. I could find a man who truly deserved her. But she wasn't just as headstrong as me – she was like me in many other ways, too. Her power rivalled mine – maybe even surpassed it. The spell never took hold of her. Not fully. She never stopped loving this man. And she never stopped hating me, for taking him from her. And then one day she told me … she told me that she was pregnant. She said she would leave Riddler's Cove, and that I would never meet my grandchild. She said … she said she would take inspiration from the spell I'd performed on the man she loved. She would break any ties the child had to the Albright coven, and that the child would never step foot in the supernatural world. She broke my heart. She broke my heart when all I did was try to be the best father I could possibly be.'

His bottle of wine was beginning to look very tempting. I'd been right to be wary of this man. He had destroyed his daughter's life, forcing her to make the only choice possible – getting herself and her child as far away from him as she could. And even now, he seemed to believe he had been acting out of love. He actually believed *he* was the injured party. What could I possibly say to a man like that?

'I used everything at my disposal to track my Abby down, and to bring she and her child back to me, where they belonged. But Abby's spell was so powerful. She had cut all family ties, all coven ties. I couldn't trace her. Almost two years after she left, the seers I employed told me she was dead. Once she died, the spell she had done to hide herself came to an end. She was cremated before I got to her. It turned out she had been hiding in the human world all along. But the child she bore … that child was still hidden. Still impossible to find. I managed to discover that the child had been a little girl, but I could find nothing more. Then, three years ago, I received further intelligence. I was told that the child had entered the Irish care system. And so I began to sift through adoption and foster records, looking for women of the right age who shared Abby's traits. I couldn't be accurate on the birth date, but I had a rough idea. The other three journalists I hired all seemed to fit the bill. They were the right age, they had all been abandoned as babies. But when they arrived here, it was clear to me that none of them were my granddaughter.'

I still wasn't sure he was deserving of the energy it would take me to speak. But my curiosity and irritation were winning me over. 'How exactly was it *clear*? How could it be? If Abby separated her child from the magical world, then she most likely found a spell to suppress that child's power, too. So you certainly couldn't tell who your granddaughter was based on whether or not they were magical. And even if they *were* the child of a witch like Abby, that doesn't necessarily mean they would have power. There are unempowered witches, aren't there?'

He poured what was left of the bottle into his glass. Probably just as well. I didn't need to be annoyed *and* drunk. That was never a good combination.

'That's exactly the sort of question my Abby would have asked,' he said. 'And that's what I was looking for in an employee. Someone who saw to the core of the matter. Someone who could never be fobbed off by a flimsy excuse. The other women I hired *seemed* like that. They had exposed corrupt politicians and dug up evidence that put the worst of people behind bars. They were truly amazing women. But once they got to Riddler's Edge, all of that changed. Aisling, this town is filled with spells. Spells to make the townsfolk look the other way. Spells to make sure that the border between here and Riddler's Cove is never crossed by the wrong person. And those reporters … they succumbed to those spells in the same way as every single human here does. You say you pestered Detective Quinn into telling you the truth? Well, none of the others did. They were fine reporters. Exemplary women. But even if my Abby hadn't an ounce of power to her name, she would have seen through it all. She would have gotten to the truth of the matter, even here. And I know that her daughter would be just the same.' He gave me a hopeful look. 'So you see now, don't you? You see that you *must* be my granddaughter. You have to be. You're the first one to have gotten this far.'

My eyes began to water. Not because I was sad for him, but because I was sad for Abby, and for her daughter. 'I'm nothing special,' I said. 'I've been doing some research, and I know that there are people out there with a small degree of power. Enough to catch glimpses of supernatural elements, but not to see the whole picture. If I'm like that, it doesn't make me your granddaughter, Arnold. And to dismiss those other girls because they had no magic was incredibly short-sighted. Like I said, Abby could have suppressed her child's power. Or the child could simply be unempowered. I have no idea why you've let this farce go on for so long. I mean, haven't witches ever heard of a DNA test?'

'It wouldn't work. Abby's spell made sure of that. But I do have a way I could tell. And that's what I'll be doing on Friday, if you'll so permit. The final test. It will tell me once and for all whether or not you're my granddaughter.'

I held my head in my hands, unable to believe what I was hearing. 'You have a test that could give you certain results? You've had this test all along? And … what? You didn't even bother to carry it out on the others? You just decided they weren't your granddaughter based on *completely* weak notions, and never even tried to prove the case either way. I'll tell you what I think, Arnold.' I felt my upper lip curl as I looked at him. 'I think you don't really *want* to find your granddaughter. Not deep down. Because otherwise, you would have done this final test on the others. You don't want to find her because you're afraid. You're afraid that she'll hate you just as much as Abby did.'

I stood up, placing my bag over my shoulder and stepping out of the booth. 'And you know what else I think? I think Abby made the right decision.

Because if I *was* your granddaughter, then I'd want nothing to do with you.'

20. The Sweet, Sweet Taste of Crud

As I marched out of the Fisherman's Friend, Arnold called me back. I ignored him and kept right on marching. I was halfway across the carpark when Pru, Greg and Jared caught up with me.

'Are you all right?' Greg asked, panting.

'Fine,' I replied. 'Just dandy. I needed some fresh air, that's all.'

The three of them stood in front of me, blocking my path. They must have moved their behinds pretty sharpish to chase after me, and yet Greg was the only one who was out of breath. Jared and Pru looked just as perfect as always.

'You're not dandy,' said Jared. 'I can tell. Anyway, who says dandy anymore?'

I sighed. '*I* say dandy. And how can you tell whether I'm dandy or not? You'd better not be reading my mind.'

'He's not,' Greg assured me. He held up another one of his gadgets. It looked like a simple black plastic ball, but seeing as it was Greg, I knew there was more to it. 'This would be turning purple if he was.'

'But hey, at least you remember my brother *is* a vampire.' Pru gave my arm a squeeze. 'Things looked so intense between you and Arnold that we were afraid he might decide to end your trial early. So … what *did* you guys talk about?'

I sat down on a bench, feeling exhausted. 'Abby. His daughter. He hasn't been looking for a reporter all this time. He's been looking for Abby's child. His granddaughter.'

Pru sat beside me, shaking her head in disbelief. 'You're not serious. I heard Abby ran away years ago, but I had no idea she had a kid. That makes this whole memory-wiping thing even *more* dubious. We should go speak to the Wayfarers about this. I'm not exactly a wunderkind when it comes to Magical Law, but I'll bet there's *something* they can do to stop him.'

Greg sat on the ground in front of us, biting his lip. 'I em … I might have guessed it was his granddaughter he was looking for. I think Grace figured it out, too. But when I told you I knew nothing about the memory wiping, I meant it. Me, Grace and Dylan were *all* in the dark about that until recently. It was only when Dylan ran into one of the reporters in Dublin and she didn't recognise him that we realised what had happened. And Dylan's doing his nut about the whole thing. I think we really do have a case to bring to the Wayfarers. Grace wants to hire you, I know she does. We should all get together and go and make an official complaint.'

I'd been close to tears when I was with Arnold, but now I was *really* having trouble holding that salty water back. I'd been here three days, and already I felt like these people were my friends. I'd never been so comfortable in all my life, and the last thing I wanted was to lose that feeling. But the practical side of my brain was ticking away, as always.

'I can't let you do that, Greg,' I said. 'Arnold is your boss. He's Grace's boss, too. Even if these Wayfarers decide to uphold a complaint against him, where will that get us? Either he'll go to jail and sell the paper, meaning you guys'll be out of a job. Or else these Wayfarers will say that he's doing nothing they can convict him of. And in that scenario, he'll probably *still* kick you out of your jobs.'

Greg shrugged. 'Grace *is* the Daily Riddler. Arnold wouldn't dream of firing her. And it's not like I don't have options. I have a lot of tech that the Wayfarers would pay me a fortune to get their hands on. I've held off selling anything because I'm a contrary son of a wizard, but believe me – I'll be quids in if I do. So don't worry about us. Worry about *you*. Do you want to work for the paper or not? Because if you do, we'll try our best to make that happen.'

Pru and Jared nodded their agreement, and the tears finally fell free. And unfortunately, I am *not* a pretty crier. I'm more of the red-faced, snotty-nosed kind of crier. But hey, at least I wouldn't have to worry about Jared trying it on with me – because *no* man would fancy me once he saw me snorting and sniffling. 'You guys are great,' I said. 'You have no idea how much it means to me that you're all on my side. But … I'm not sure *what* I want. I think I might just go for a walk on the beach to clear my head.'

Jared reached out a hand, pulling me to standing. 'Well then a walk you shall have, with the most wonderful escorts a lady could ask for.'

Pru rolled her eyes and pulled her brother away from me. 'She means a walk *alone,* Casanova.'

He frowned. 'She does? She doesn't even want *me* to go with her?'

I wiped my face and looked at the steps that ran from the Fisherman's Friend carpark, down onto the sandy shore. The waves were lapping, the moon was shining. It was a beautiful night. The sort of night any woman would want to spend with a guy as handsome as Jared.

'Not even you, I'm afraid,' I said. 'I have a lot to think about. But I won't be long, so if you see Fuzz, tell him he'd better not be hogging the bed when I get back.'

≈

I pulled off my boots and socks, kneading my toes into the damp sand. Sure, it was a chilly night, but I couldn't help myself. I had always loved the seaside. It played a key part in my sexy-man-with-a-lighthouse fantasies, after all.

I tried to think through everything that had happened with Arnold, but instead I found my mind turning to Bathsheba's murder, and the article I was going to write. I really *did* want it to be a comprehensive piece. I wanted to portray all points of view, even if I didn't agree with them all. The hatred Vlad's Boys felt towards dayturners. The sweet, friendly Bathsheba I'd met on the train. The undying love her husband felt for her.

There were more people I wanted to interview, too. I wanted to speak with Miriam a bit longer. Out of all the staff I'd spoken with, it seemed that she was closest to Gunnar. With his parents, and Gunnar himself, refusing to speak, Miriam's words might be the closest I could get to peeking inside Gunnar's mind.

As if I'd conjured her by my thoughts alone, I suddenly saw Miriam a little further along the beach. She was standing close to the water, speaking into her phone. I quickened my steps, tiny seashell-shards and pebbles sticking into my feet as I ran.

I was about ten feet away from her when I heard her side of the conversation clearly.

'I know, right? He's actually taking the fall for me.' She giggled. 'I told you he was the perfect guy to get on board. I mean, even *I* didn't think he'd be dumb enough to get a tattoo when I suggested it, but he did it straight away.'

I stopped, gulped, and ducked behind a nearby rock. Sure, I knew I'd probably done so way too late. She was bound to have sensed movement. The clever thing to have done would have been to casually walk by, say, 'Hey Miriam,' like I hadn't got a care in the world, and keep on walking. Instead I was stooping behind a damp rock – not a very large one, either – and deciding whether it would be better to make a run for it, or to phone for help. Well done me. If anyone from the Secret Service is reading this, I should be back on the job market any day now, so give me a call.

'Who's there?' Miriam called out.

Okay, maybe all I could hope for right now was a godsend. Or a goddess send. I didn't know the phone number of anyone in town, but I had the number of the Daily Riddler stored. Maybe Grace would be back by now. I dialled, stuck my phone back into my pocket, then stood up.

'Hey there.' I smiled and waved. 'It's Miriam, isn't it?'

She smiled back, but hers had even less warmth than my own. 'You know I'm reading your mind right now, right?'

'I … why would you do that?' I barely had the sentence out when she disappeared from my view.

All the research in the world couldn't have prepared me for what happened next. I knew vampires could move fast, but I had no idea what that would be like when I saw it in action. Or *didn't* see it in action. Before I knew it, Miriam was standing behind me, her teeth against my neck, her hand pulling my phone from my pocket, killing the call before throwing it aside.

'I know you heard me,' she said. 'That's the good thing about humans – they have no idea how to shield their thoughts. Right now you're wondering how on earth Detective Quinn managed to overlook me.' She moved her lips to my ear, her sharp teeth pricking my skin. 'You think he's grumpy but sexy. Yeah, I can see that. He's also blind as a bat when it comes down to discovering the people behind Vlad's Boys. He overlooked *me* because I'm not a boy.' She giggled. 'Classic misdirection, am I right? Most of our best assassins are women. We recruit dumb young guys like Gunnar to do the grunt work, and to take the fall if need be.'

Thoughts of struggle faded as quickly as they began. Greg had told me mind-readers were a rarity among vampires. Not quite as rare as I wished.

And my research had also told me that those vampires who *could* read human minds also tended to be more powerful in general. Which meant that Miriam was bound to be far stronger and faster than I could ever hope to be.

There had to be some way out of this, though. Maybe Grace would try and call me back and get worried when I didn't answer. Or perhaps Jared, Pru and Greg would come looking for me. But I couldn't see or hear them anywhere near the beach, so it was more likely that they were continuing with their Pru-inclusive boys' night out.

I caught sight of the lighthouse, far along the shore. Maybe Detective Quinn was in there now, looking through a telescope (he had everything *else* my sexy lighthouse-fantasy man had, so why not that?). He'd spy me down here and … what? He probably wouldn't come to my rescue. I mean, he hated my guts, so why *not* let me get murdered by a vampire? It wasn't as though I actually *cared* what he thought of me. I wasn't a needy woman. But he could at least show *some* sort of decency and try to rescue me, instead of just standing there in his lighthouse enjoying the show.

'For the love of Dracula! What is *with* your brain? You realise you're getting annoyed with a guy because you've *imagined* he's looking out through a telescope at you right now.' She shook her head. 'Dear me, humans are dumb. But listen, I have things to do tonight, so I'm just going to get on with it and murder you, okay? And I might take a little drink of your blood, first. It's a while since I've eaten.'

I didn't want to be the woman who just stood there while a vampire drank from her and plotted her murder, really I didn't. But what was I going to do about it? Sure, I'd taken a few self-defence classes, but I didn't think I'd hold up too well against Miriam. Also, she could probably just compel me to be docile even if I tried.

'Yes,' she said, her teeth sinking into my neck. 'I could.'

Ahem. This is the kind of paragraph that needs some preparatory throat clearing. Ahem. Quite a lot of it, it turns out. Because in the same way as I hadn't been prepared for the reality of Miriam's strength, I also hadn't been prepared for the experience of being bitten. And it was – ahem – it was … well, it was euphoric. Something I could definitely get used to, if she didn't decide to drain me dry. I was feeling energised by the whole thing, truth be told. I was feeling like, as soon as she took a break, I might just have summoned the strength to fight her off. I was–

'Ugh!' She pushed me away, throwing up on the sand.

Hmm. I should probably be insulted. And I would be later on, no doubt. But for the time being, she was vomiting a *lot,* and I decided to take the opportunity to scarper. I didn't even stop to pick up my shoes. I just ran towards the steps that would lead me back to the Fisherman's Friend carpark, my lungs burning with the effort.

I was about three feet away from those steps when I was pulled back, hard and swift. Before I could figure out what was happening, I was lying face down in the water, with Miriam's hands around my throat. 'What the hell *are* you? Your blood just made me throw up.'

'Yeah, I noticed that,' I said through a mouthful of sand and salt water. 'Say, maybe we should talk about it. We could figure out what's up with my blood. You could tell me a little more about Vlad's Boys. Y'know – some nice girly back and forth.'

She smacked me hard across the face. 'Listen, sweetie, I'm aware that some villains like to do a bit of a tell-all before they kill their victim. And I can see the benefit. A bit of catharsis. Get all of the stress out by unloading it on someone you're soon going to shut up forever. But I *think* I'll forgo that, seeing as I'm still feeling slightly nauseous. Oh, and if you're worried about me getting caught, then don't. I've been in your head. I know how upset you are about this whole *Is Abby my mammy* thing. And it's probably fairly obvious to anyone who can't read your pathetic thoughts, too. So I'm going to put a whole heap of stones in your pockets before I drown you. They'll think you were so depressed that you did it to yourself.'

I was surprised she said *before* she drowned me, because as far as I could tell, it was already happening. 'They'll see the bite marks!' I spluttered. 'They'll know I didn't drown myself.'

'My bite has healing qualities, Sherlock. The marks will have disappeared by the time they find you. No one will ever know you've been bitten.' She shuddered. 'I wish *I* could undo the memory of that little interaction. You taste like crud. No, you taste like the crud that the rest of the crud has crudded out.'

'No need to be insulting,' I said in a somewhat garbled tone. I felt her weight lift off me then, but before I could move she was back again with the promised stones. How nice – a woman of her word. I felt her stuff them into my pockets, then lift me up and move me into deeper water.

This was it, my last hurrah. I'd never imagined it would be a hurrah-filled hurrah, to be honest. I'd imagined myself dying alone in my flat, half a dozen cats feasting on me until someone finally complained to the building manager about the smell. At least this was a bit more exciting.

I struggled and flailed for a while, and then there was the excruciating discomfort that being drowned entails, but after a few minutes of all that good stuff, my thoughts began to drift away …

21. The Kiss of Life

'I'm kind of disappointed,' said a husky voice. 'I was hoping I'd get to enjoy that for a little bit longer.'

My eyelids were heavy as mud, and my ears felt like someone had shoved a scream inside. My mouth was wet, tasting of brine. I forced my eyes open, sat up and wiped my face. Jared was looking down at me, smiling. His face looked as wet as mine felt. His T-shirt, too. Actually, *all* of him was wet. Fuzz was sitting next to him, not quite soaked through, but definitely a bit damp.

My brain finally caught up with what was happening, and I said, 'Wait – you just saved my life?'

Jared grinned, while Fuzz rubbed up against me and purred.

'Well, it wasn't exactly a chore. I did enjoy the whole mouth-to-mouth resuscitation thing, I must admit. And the fight I had with Miriam was also oddly satisfying. I should probably speak with a therapist about that. Unresolved issues with my mother, perhaps? Anyway.' He shook his head, droplets falling from his bleached hair onto my legs. Dear goddess, a wet man had never looked so attractive. 'Much as I wish I could take all the credit, you have Fuzz here to thank, too.'

I picked the cat up, stroking his black fur. A wave of warmth seemed to rush from him into me, and it was so comforting that I felt as if my body was instantly recovering from the whole almost-drowning debacle. And, whilst I still couldn't hear a word he said, I had the uncanny feeling that Fuzz was saying *something,* and that whatever it was, it was lovely.

'I heard him scratching to get into your bedroom,' Jared went on. 'And I know you said *not* to let him hog the bed, but he is awfully cute. Y'know – for a creature who hates vampires with a passion. Anyway, as soon as I let him in, he walked over to the telescope and started meowing like crazy. I took a look and … well, y'know, I *can* move super-fast when I want to. Just another of my attributes you might want to consider the next time you turn down my offer of a date.'

My heart began to beat a little wildly. Jared with a telescope, seeing my struggle and coming to my rescue. Okay, so he didn't live in a lighthouse, but the Vander Inn *was* kind of sexy. Y'know, if you overlooked the doilies.

I glanced down at the cat. It was safer than staring at Jared with my tongue hanging out.

'You've managed to get into my room with the door closed before,' I said.

Fuzz head-bumped me, purring louder than ever. What the criminy did all of this mean? Did the cat *know* I was in trouble? Was this whole witch-familiar thing really happening? Didn't that require me to *be* a witch? I shook my head. Such thoughts could wait. After all, I had a whole two days left to mull them over before I lost all memory of my time here. 'Where's Miriam?'

Jared pointed up the beach. Miriam was standing next to Greg, stock-still, while he held that sparkly purple wand of his out towards her. Pru and her mother were a little further up the beach, leading a group of people towards us. Some of them were dressed like Gretel.

'Pru called Greg while I came here to rescue you,' Jared explained. 'He got here just in time, and Pru got on the phone to the Wayfarers in the meantime. I was struggling to hold Miriam in check *and* do the whole glorious kiss of life thing, so it was a good thing I had some help. That wand of Greg's must be pretty powerful. I don't think I've ever seen a wizard manage a freezing spell before.'

'It's an OAP,' I said, giggling a little manically. Greg the wizard had frozen Miriam the vampire with an OAP, while another vampire had given me mouth-to-mouth. Not only had he given me mouth-to-mouth, but he'd done so without telling me I tasted like crud. I was trying to think of something sensible to say, when I saw flashing lights in the Fisherman's Friend carpark. Next came the slam of a car door, followed by Detective Quinn rushing down onto the beach.

'About time too,' Jared muttered, his jaw tense. 'I heard he was having a date with his ex-fiancée tonight. Trying to rekindle the old flame. I mean, sure, we all need time off, but … how could he have overlooked Miriam? You could have died tonight, because of his ineptitude.'

A strange feeling crashed into my chest. It felt like *I* was being insulted. Which was ridiculous, right? But I had the sudden need to defend Detective Quinn as strongly as I might defend myself. 'He wasn't the only one trying to find the killer. You might as well blame all of these Wayfarer people, too, if you're going to start throwing blame around.'

Instead of acting insulted by my words, Jared smiled softly down at me. 'You have a heart of gold, do you know that? Come on, I want to get you home and warmed up. And my mother will want to mollycoddle you for days to come.'

I stood up, glancing at Detective Quinn. 'I should probably tell him what happened, first.'

Jared wrapped an arm around my waist, steadying me. It was a good thing, too, because I'd stood up far more quickly than I should have, and I was experiencing a headrush.

'Of course,' he said. 'What was I thinking? But I'll stay by your side, if that's okay. I want to make sure you don't wear yourself out.'

≈

I sat at my desk the next day, writing up the events of the night before and expanding the story. I hoped Grace was a quick editor, because this piece was constantly evolving. As long as nothing else surprising happened in the meantime, I should be finished by the end of the day.

She'd been out the night before, and hadn't heard my call. But it had apparently gone to voicemail for a few seconds before Miriam threw my phone away, and the beginning of our conversation had been clear. If Miriam *had* murdered me, she would have been the chief suspect. I could lie to you and tell you I found comfort in that thought, but I'm not quite so noble. I was *very* glad to be alive.

I was also glad that my mobile phone was alive. Greg had found it on the sand and managed to repair any water damage. Who knew a wizard could be so useful?

The atmosphere in the Daily Riddler was doing nothing to help my writing speed along. Malachy had brought me coffee and croissants, Greg had brought me coffee and doughnuts. Edward had brought me green tea and overnight oats, and

Roarke had brought me chai tea, cinnamon rolls and a book of puzzles. I mean, sure, I ate and drank it all – I was hardly going to be rude – but all the niceness was a little embarrassing. Back at the Daily Dubliner, the most anyone sent my way was a grunt.

The precious princess treatment in the office was nothing compared to what it had been like at the Vander Inn, though. Jared, Pru and Nollaig had been fussing over me so much that I'd been glad to escape to work.

It was about eleven a.m. when Detective Quinn marched into the office. Judging by the look on his face, he wasn't here to bring me a snack. 'You look recovered,' he said, dragging a chair over next to me.

I shrugged. 'I've been reading up on vampire bites. Apparently they can be rather energising. You're not looking too well-rested yourself, though.'

'I'll head off to bed once I've seen Greg. I need him, and badly. But I want to talk to you first, Miss Smith. I know you told me everything Miriam said last night, but maybe there was something you missed. Did she mention Bathsheba at all?'

'Nope, not a jot. Why? And why do you need Greg? Wait, don't tell me – you only want him for his computer skills. I mean, he'll probably be a little disappointed if you don't buy him dinner first, but …'

The detective rolled his eyes. 'There's something wrong with you, do you know that? Last night a vampire almost murdered you, and today you're joking around as if it never happened. And speaking of last night … you and Mr Montague looked awfully close.'

I wrinkled my nose, sipping the last of my chai tea. 'Mr who now?'

'Jared. You let a guy fawn all over you when you don't even know his name?'

Okay, I was no longer feeling jokey. I resisted the urge to slam my cup on my desk – or better yet, throw its contents at him. Why was this man so ridiculously rude *all* the time? 'Come on.' I stood up, smoothing down my jeans (no, they did not need to be smoothed down, but if my hands were doing that, then they weren't throwing things). 'Greg's in his office. What do you want him for?'

Detective Quinn sighed. 'Miriam's admitted to all of the murders except Bathsheba's. She says she liked Bathsheba too much to kill her, and she insists that it must have been Gunnar. I've heard about Greg's new aura-matching program. Maybe it can tell me if Miriam is telling the truth.'

≈

I stood behind the two men while they stared at Greg's computer screen. Sure, the detective threw me a look now and then that told me he'd rather I went elsewhere. But if he wanted me out, he'd have to ask. I was having far too much fun watching him fail to grasp the obvious.

'It can't be right, though,' he said to Greg for the tenth time.

'It *is* right,' Greg insisted. 'I took a photo of Miriam last night. Her aura is *nowhere* in all of the telekinetic energy that occurred during Bathsheba's murder. If I were a betting man, I'd put every penny I had on Miriam being innocent. Of Bathsheba's murder, at least. My program says she *did* murder the other three dayturners on the train.'

The detective kicked the leg of the desk. 'So she's telling the truth? Okay, well then it has to be Gunnar. He has to have been the one who murdered Bathsheba.'

Greg shook his head. 'I don't think so. I ran his aura against Bathsheba's murder scene and got a zero percent match.'

'Well, run it again.'

Greg pulled a packet of crisps from his pocket, opened it, and began to crunch loudly. 'I ran it three times,' he said between mouthfuls. 'I'm not going to get a different result running it a fourth. Look, I know you want to hang something on Gunnar, and I can't blame you. The kid is scum. But you might have to accept that all you're going to be able to do him for is being a member of a hate group.'

'How much time in Witchfield will that get him?' I asked.

The detective began to grind his teeth. 'Not enough. Dayturners were only granted equal rights a few weeks ago. And so far, Judge Redvein has been way too lenient when it comes to handing down hate crime sentences. She seems to think things will take a while to settle, and that we should all just be patient. She'll give him two years for being a member of Vlad's Boys, and he'll probably get out after one.' He leant down over Greg. 'Have you run everyone else's aura photo against Bathsheba's murder scene? All the passengers? All the staff?'

Greg scraped the last crisps out of his bag, chewed them slowly, and licked the crumbs from his hands. 'Every single one,' he confirmed. 'I'm telling you – no one on that train murdered Bathsheba.'

22. The Things We Do For Love

I hovered at the edge of the dining room. Nollaig was playing cards with Grace and a rather dashing looking werewolf. Pru was telling fortunes at a table by the window. Malachy was dishing out amazing food, and Greg was playing barman to at least two dozen guests. This was it, the party that they swore was *not* my goodbye party.

When Greg insisted on walking me straight home after work, I should have known that something was going on. And I *definitely* should have known when all the lights in the Vander Inn were turned off. But I'm ashamed to say that it was only when everyone leapt up and shouted, 'Surprise!' that I cottoned on to the reality of the situation. I know what you're thinking – I'm the *perfect* person to call when you need a crime solved.

The party had been Jared's idea. He wanted me to meet as many local supernaturals as possible. He seemed to think that, the more people who spoke up for me, the less likely Arnold was to try and send me back to the Daily Dubliner. For a couple of hours he did the rounds, telling everyone how I'd tracked down Miriam all by myself.

'Ash almost lost her life in the pursuit of justice,' I heard him say to a middle-aged wizard at one stage. 'Just think what a boon someone like her would be to our town.'

He was laying it on thick, that was for sure. And I really *was* grateful for the efforts he was making. But the thing was, I was feeling a little on the antsy side. Whoever had murdered Bathsheba was still out there, and I'd probably never get a chance to write the real story. What I'd printed out before I left the office that evening felt so unfinished.

No one else seemed to feel that way, though – or if they did, they were hiding it well. The party was getting more raucous by the minute. Drinks were flowing, and someone had brought a karaoke machine. Roarke turned out to be just as talented a singer as he was a puzzle-writer, and he began to belt out rock tunes at the top of his lungs.

Jared moved on from the wizard, and began to schmooze an attractive young witch. Sure I could hear him mention my name while they talked, but I could also see the way his eyes strayed to her cleavage. Not that she seemed to mind. She was doing that whole arm-touching and hair-tossing thing. The sort of thing you read about in articles on how to flirt. Obviously *I* have never tried to put such advice into action.

Either Detective Quinn wasn't invited, or he had declined to come. I hoped I'd see him at least once more before tomorrow evening. Sure, he was a grumpy sod, but he was also the only one who told me the truth. If it hadn't been for him, I'd be seriously questioning my sanity by now.

As the night wore on, my edginess only grew. Jared finally stopped chatting up women and joined me on the staircase, where I was hanging out with Fuzz.

'Sorry I haven't had much of a chance to chat with you. I've been trying to make your case to the movers and shakers. And I *might* have been trying to make you jealous by flirting with the last three of those movers and shakers.' He shoulder-bumped me. 'Did it work?'

'You're full of it,' I replied with a wry grin.

'Ah, but full of what? Awesomeness? Heroism? Sexiness? I'm not just doing this for you, you know. I'm doing it for Greg and Pru, too. They like you a lot. And Grace has been writing every single article for the paper all by herself for the last thirty years. She could probably do with some help.'

Fuzz let out a loud meow, as though he were agreeing.

'I don't quite get what it is you think you're doing, though. I've already told you guys my opinion on all of this. Arnold doesn't *want* to hire a reporter. He wants to find his granddaughter. You might be able to force him not to wipe my memory, but if I don't pass this final test tomorrow, then he's not going to keep me on – no matter what anyone says to him.'

Jared grabbed my hand, and I flinched. His palm felt cool, but that was probably down to the whole undead thing he had going on. 'Sorry,' he said, dropping my hand. 'But I just … I've been thinking this through a lot. When I saw you and Miriam last night, it was like a kick to the gut. I might not know you very long, but I know I *want* to know you better. So I was thinking – even if you *don't* stay on at the paper, that doesn't mean you can't still stay here, does it? At this stage, Arnold's not going to get away with wiping your memory. So you could just … stay. And if you did, then we could go out, get to know each other.'

I twirled a strand of my hair and eyed him, wondering just how serious he was. I'd seen him in action at this very party, and I was old enough to know that I didn't want a drama-filled relationship. 'Tell you what,' I said. 'If I'm still here this time next week, I'll go out with you. One date.'

He grabbed my hand again. 'Well now you've given me even *more* incentive to make sure you stay. Come on. Do the rounds with me. Show every supernatural in Riddler's Edge just how fabulous you are.'

I stood up, gently pulling my hand from his and gathering Fuzz into my arms. 'Maybe in a while. I'm feeling a little overwhelmed right now. I'm going to head upstairs for a few minutes.'

'But you'll be back?'

I nodded. 'I'll be back.'

≈

I opened up my one suitcase, and neatly packed all of my clothes. I kept one outfit out for tomorrow. My final day, probably. Because no matter what Jared said, I knew there was nothing any of them could do to change Arnold's mind.

Abby Albright, the woman who most likely was *not* my mother, had left the magical world for a reason. She knew what sort of man her father was, and she also knew better than to try to change him. I wouldn't put it past the old guy to go ahead and wipe my memory, and then wipe a little bit of everyone else's memory so that they'd forget I'd ever been here.

And even though I was falling in love with Riddler's Edge, I wasn't so sure that losing my memory of it would be all that bad an outcome.

Because if I was going to have to go back to Dublin without finding out who murdered Bathsheba, then I'd rather not have it eating away at me forever.

I soon packed everything that could be packed, but I still wasn't in the mood to go back downstairs. Fuzz jumped up onto my lap, head-bumping my belly in the cutest way.

'Whatever happens, Fuzz, promise me that you won't let me forget *you.* Sneak onto the train. Sneak into my bag. Do all the sneaky things you've got to do, but just … stay with me.'

As I spoke, I realised just how deeply I meant every word. I loved this cat even more than I loved Riddler's Edge. In a few short days he'd managed to make himself a permanent – and necessary – feature in my life. If I had to leave him behind, I thought my heart might just well break.

'I know you'll find a way,' I said, snuggling closer to him. 'Because you know by now that I'm *kind* of in love with you. And I dunno about you, Fuzz, but I would do *anything* for love.'

The cat purred and head-bumped me again.

'That's all Arnold was doing, I guess,' I rambled on. 'He was doing it for love. He loved his daughter so much – too much – that he wanted to protect her from the world. He …' I abruptly stopped talking, as a thought entered my mind.

I stood up, placing the cat on the bed. 'Sorry, Fuzz,' I said. 'But I've just had a thought and … well … I've got to go and annoy Detective Grumpy

Pants about it. I'll leave the door open so you can get out, okay? Not that you actually *need* it to be left open, my crafty little cat.'

Fuzz began to lick his paws – a sure sign that he was quite all right on his own – so I ran from the room, sped down the stairs and searched for Greg.

≈

'I know you're home,' I said, banging on the door of the lighthouse and talking through the letterbox. 'It's night time, and your car is here. I seriously doubt you'd go out without your car at night if you could help it.'

The door was jerked open, and Detective Quinn stood in front of me, wearing nothing but a towel. 'I wasn't ignoring you, you nutjob!' he barked. 'I was in the bloody shower.'

'Oh.' I did my best not to let my eyes linger on his upper body. Yeah, it was a little on the pale side, but it was ripped. Seriously ripped. 'Well, what do you expect me to think? I assumed you were being just as rude as you usually are. Are you em … are you alone?'

His hands shielded his eyes, and he stepped back into the hallway. 'Of course I'm alone. Come in, you idiot. Before I get a rash.'

I stepped inside. 'You mean a rash because of the darkness, right? Not a rash because I'm irritating?'

'I'm thinking both are equally possible,' he drawled. 'So why *are* you banging on my door in the middle of the night? Shouldn't you be off enjoying the party that lover boy is throwing for you?'

He reached a hand up to towel his hair, and my eyes followed the motion. A little hungrily, I guess, because he suddenly said, 'You know what – hold off on whatever you're about to tell me until I get dressed.'

'Good idea,' I said with a gulp as he walked towards the stairs. 'I'll put some coffee on.'

≈

Five minutes later, I was still pawing confusedly at his coffee machine. I had pressed the button that I figured I ought to press, and fiddled about with some levers that looked like they needed fiddling with, but nothing seemed to be happening.

'What are you doing?' He appeared behind me, fully clothed, shaking his head and pressing a button that I'd already pressed. 'You need to switch it on, genius.'

'I already pressed that button, though,' I said, then trailed off as the machine went into action. 'Or maybe I just pressed one that looked like it. I mean, it's great to have a coffee-maker that looks all sleek and shiny and everything, but a label here or there wouldn't go amiss.'

He sighed. 'I'll get onto the manufacturer. Why are you here, anyway?'

'Oh. Yeah. That. I was just wondering … did you do anything to discount Donald from your suspect list?'

His eyes bulged. 'Donald? Listen, I know there are some detectives who think it's always the spouse. But trust me, this time it's definitely not the spouse.'

'Are you sure? I mean, did you even go down that avenue?'

'No. Why would I? Vlad's Boys were behind the rest of the murders, and they were behind this one, too. I just have to find the proof.' He sat into a stool at the kitchen counter. 'You never saw Donald and Bathsheba together. I did. They were the real thing, Miss Smith. True love. I already told you how they only turned into vampires because they couldn't bear to be without each other. He could no sooner kill his wife than he could himself.'

I sat down next to him. 'Detective … I can see the twelve zillion photos of you and the beauty queen all over this lighthouse, so I *know* you know what love is. And love like that – big love – that's *exactly* why I think it was Donald. Bathsheba couldn't bear being a dayturner. She told me as much on the train. She said she hated her condition. And she told me that her husband made her the coffee in her vacuum flask. Did you even test that flask?'

He shot me the sort of look that seemed to say: *I didn't think I could find you more irritating than I already do, but it turns out I was wrong.*

'Miss Smith, why in the world didn't you mention this flask before?'

My mouth hung open and I shook my head. 'I did!' I spat. 'I mentioned it just before you had Gretel shoo me out of the dining car. I assumed that even though you hated me on sight, you would have at least followed a viable lead.'

He stood up and gripped the countertop, his skin turning even paler than usual. Well, now I had no idea *what* he was thinking, but seeing as he was probably thinking it about me, then I doubted it was pleasant.

'I don't hate you,' he said, his voice hoarse. 'I thought I explained already. I was keeping my distance because I was annoyed about what Arnold was doing.'

I gritted my teeth. He wasn't *that* annoyed. If he was, he would have been at the party tonight, doing what Jared and the others were doing – trying to find a way that I could stay. 'Whatever. Look, why are we arguing about this?' I said, brushing my irritation aside. 'Did you test the flask or not?'

He swallowed. 'I … I don't even remember *seeing* a vacuum flask. I mean, I vaguely remember you babbling about something when I was telling

Gretel to get you out of the dining car but … no. We didn't take a flask into evidence. Are you sure you saw one? I mean, we went over the place with a magical tooth comb. Maybe you imagined it.'

'Oh, you did *not* just say that.' I stood up and glared at him. 'I've been accused of imagining things all my life, Detective Quinn. Those people were wrong to accuse me, and you're wrong now. There *was* a flask. And if you're struggling to think of where it could have gone, then I suggest you go into a different line of work. I've only known about this world for a few days, and even I know how quickly vampires can move, how they can vaporize themselves, get in and out of anywhere without being seen. Just remind me again? What manner of supernatural *is* Donald?'

He clenched his jaw. 'It wasn't Donald. I'm sorry, but it just wasn't.'

I opened up my bag, my hands shaking with anger. 'Greg let me borrow his laptop,' I said, trying to keep my voice calm while I pulled the computer from my bag and switched it on. It booted up quickly, and I found Greg's photo folder, then opened up a picture of Donald and copied it into the aura-matching program. 'Greg used one of his aura filters when he took Donald's photo,' I explained. 'He had no intention of testing Donald against the murder scene. He wanted to see if grief had an effect on a person's aura.'

I glanced at Detective Quinn while I worked. His jaw was *still* clenched, and I could tell that he wanted me to be wrong more than anything. Had I really believed this conversation would go differently? I knew he hated Vlad's Boys, and I couldn't say I blamed him, but I had hoped that he would at least take me seriously.

I had defended him to Arnold. To Jared, too. And right now I had no idea why. Maybe he *was* inept. Maybe he couldn't see far enough past his hatred of Vlad's Boys to be able to do his job. I quickly finished typing in the commands Greg had written down for me, and looked up at the detective as the aura-matching program began to run. 'We'll soon know whether I'm *imagining* things or not. Won't we?'

As I spoke, his face was growing paler than ever. I looked back at the screen, and I could see why. It read: *One hundred percent match.*

He swallowed, took a set of keys from a bowl on the counter and tossed them my way. 'I'm going to go grab my night gear. Start the car.'

≈

'Explain to me again why I'm driving?' I asked as I sped erratically along the forest road. It was ages since I'd driven, but I doubted regular practice would improve my skills behind the wheel.

'Because I have a million calls to make,' he replied agitatedly. 'I need to get a search warrant. I need to get the Wayfarers there, too, in case Donald tries any tricks. I'll need to get a Potions' expert, as well. Because even if we do find the Thermos, we'll need to test it for Night potion. And I'll want to have that done straight away, so I'll have to try and get someone into the lab. And–'

He realised that I had slowed to a stop, and his babbling halted along with me. 'What? Why are you stopping? We need to get there. We need to search his house.'

I turned off the engine and looked at him. 'Detective, do you really want to go off half-cocked again?'

'Half-cocked?' His voice went a little high-pitched. Oh dear, I did seem to be developing a habit of saying exactly what he didn't want to hear. I might feel bad about it, sometime in the future when he stopped being a pig-headed idiot. 'Again? You mean like with Gunnar, right? You know what, you really *will* fit in at Arnold's paper, seeing as all the old goat ever does is accuse me of being bad at my job.'

'Whoa,' I said, glaring at him. 'If you want people to stop accusing you of being bad at your job, then maybe you should get your head out of your behind, stop feeling sorry for yourself and get on with being *good* at your job.'

I bit my lip, gripped the steering wheel, and wondered if I should just get out of his car right now – because if I didn't, he was probably going to throw me out.

'I guess I deserved that,' he said quietly.

I cleared my throat. It seemed safer than responding.

'I do feel sorry for myself,' he went on, his voice still quiet. 'I never thought I'd be the sort of guy for self-pity, and yet here I am.' He turned in his seat, and I got the feeling that, somewhere beneath all of that night gear, he was looking right at me. 'Someday I'll tell you how I became a dayturner. Maybe then you'll get why I hate Vlad's Boys so much. But you're right – I need to stop feeling sorry for myself, because it *is* affecting my job. Miss Smith … Aisling … how do you want to play this?'

I looked at him. 'Whatever Donald did, I believe he did it for love. So I'd like to try, oh, I dunno – maybe talking to him.' I held my hands up. 'Before you argue with me, hear me out. You can call your people, have them on standby. But I really believe that talking to him is the best way to go. And in a few days' time I'll be miles away from here, working for the Daily Dubliner again with no idea that any of this ever happened. But you'll remember. You'll remember tonight. So tell me, how do you want to remember it? You want to recall yourself as the guy who couldn't at least give me *one* win before I get magicked back to Normalsville?'

For some reason, he was shaking a little. He seemed to be … no … he couldn't be. 'Are you *laughing* at me?'

A great big bellow escaped his mouth. 'I'm trying very hard not to. But you really are hilarious. Come on. Start the engine back up. We'll do it your way.'

I held out a hand and wiggled my little finger. 'Pinky swear?'

I was *sure* I saw him do an eye-roll behind those sunglasses, but he caught my finger in his. 'Pinky swear – you madwoman. And by the way, I'm going to do my best to make sure you get to stay.'

≈

All the lights were blazing in Donald's house. I could see him through his window, sitting by the fire, sipping a glass of something red and viscous and crying into a photo album.

He looked up as though he knew we were there, and left his seat. A moment later, he drew open the door.

'I know why you're here,' he said. 'And I'll come peacefully.'

The detective's eyes grew round. If this were a less upsetting situation, I might be feeling the urge to gloat.

'She asked me to do it,' Donald went on. 'But that's not really what matters, is it? I heard that a young man from Vlad's Boys is your chief suspect. I know what they are. I know what they stand for. Gunnar was always horrible to my wife, and that group *do* poison dayturners, I know they do. But even if Gunnar and his group killed those other dayturners, they didn't kill my wife. I just wanted one more night, here with my photos of my Bathsheba, before I handed myself in.' He gave us a shaky smile. 'She made me promise not to follow her to the afterlife,' he said. 'That's why she insisted on the Night potion. So it would look like the other deaths. No one would know I did it, and I could go and live my life without her.' He wiped his eyes and blinked back tears. 'But I don't think she knew what she was asking of me. I can't let that young man take the fall – no matter what sort of person he is.'

23. The Test

It was late on Friday afternoon, and I was sitting across from Grace, twiddling my thumbs while she checked her make-up in the mirror. I wasn't sure why it needed so much attention, seeing as it looked just as perfect as always.

'Just tell me you hated my story,' I said. 'I'm a big girl. I can take the criticism.'

She looked up, her eyes wide. 'Why would I tell you that? It would be a lie.' She put her mirror on the desk and pushed it across to me. 'In case you were wondering, I wasn't checking my make-up,' she said. 'It's another Aurameter. Different design.'

I picked it up and looked into it. Instead of my reflection (which was, no doubt, absolutely horrendous) I saw Grace, surrounded by that same golden light.

'I still can't see any power when I look at you,' she said. 'But everything that you've done since you've been here … it made me *want* to see something, so badly.' Her long lashes fluttered. 'You look so much like her, but so did the other three girls. It was never about looks. They might have had the right colouring, but they were nothing like Abby. You are.'

I looked down at my hands. I didn't want to hear that I reminded her of Abby. Because the more I heard it, the more I might dare to hope. And to hope I was related to a dead witch? That was the sort of hope that was going to bring nothing but misery.

'Anyway,' she said, her voice sounding strained. 'That hardly matters, does it? Arnold chose you for the same reason he chose the others – because you *are* like Abby. He, um … he read your piece.' She reached for a handkerchief. 'Excuse me. Allergies. Anyway … it really was more than satisfactory.'

'Oh.' I turned the latest Aurameter over in my hands. 'Good. Satisfactory is … good.'

She nodded. 'Yes. Yes, it is. Now. He wants to meet with you again this evening. For the final test. It'll take place at his home in Riddler's Cove. I thought … well … I thought maybe I could accompany you?'

I gave her a grateful smile. 'That's a nice thought, Grace. But I need to do this alone. And, em … is there anything else you want me to work on for the rest of the day?'

She shook her head, golden curls bouncing. 'I think you've earned an afternoon off, don't you?'

≈

I didn't know how to feel as I walked through the Wandering Wood. All my life I'd convinced myself I didn't care who my mother was, or why she'd left me in front of the hospital. I told myself that what mattered was who I was, and who I became. I told myself that I was perfectly fine on my own.

Sure, the fact that so many foster families had dumped me had probably made me a *little* unsure that I was perfectly fine. But it had made me get used to the fact that I was born to be alone.

Apparently there were only a few ways to make it through the Wandering Wood without straying. It wasn't an *evil* wood, Pru assured me. It just liked to have a little fun now and then. You would always get to where you were going, but you might take a little longer than you thought. Pru knew of a path that would get me there in the shortest time possible – but she warned me that, whilst it was the shortest path, it wasn't going to be completely without wonder.

One minute I was looking at a pond on my left side, and another minute that exact same pond was on my right. Trees seemed to follow me, too. Even though Pru had done her best to prepare me, I still jumped every time the scenery changed.

She had offered to come with me. As had Nollaig, Jared, Greg and Malachy. But just as when

Grace asked me, I'd insisted on going it alone. I had decided exactly what I was going to say to Arnold, and I knew that if they were with me, it would be all the harder to see that decision through. The last thing I needed was a fit of the waterworks.

When I saw an oak shift from my left to my right, I looked up at it and said, 'Hey, tree. I'm not at *all* concerned that this whole forest can move about willy-nilly.'

The tree stayed still, but I had the eerie feeling that it was giving me a wink.

In all, taking Pru's path took ten minutes, and I was now staring through the trees at the narrow lane that led up to the main street of Riddler's Cove. I could hear the bustle from the market place. I could see kids riding about on brooms as though it were a perfectly normal thing to do. As I walked along, I even saw a woman repaint her front door without a paintbrush. She simply waved her hands, muttered some words that I assumed were a spell and … *tada*! A red door was now a purple one.

I knew that I needed to take the road that led east off the market square, and that Arnold's house would be the third on the left side of that road. But for some reason, I found myself lingering in the market. Sure, the stalls were fascinating, but I knew it wasn't only that. It was … well, I guess it was that I was suddenly frightened to death of what would happen once I got to Arnold's.

'Ash?'

I looked up at the sound of my name being called. It was the Amazonian goddess from the train. 'Gretel?' I gave her a shaky smile. 'How are you?'

'Oh, I'm great,' she said, cleaning up a spot of tea she'd just spilled down the front of her outfit. 'Apart from the fact that this is the third breastplate I've spilled something on this month.' She looked at the ring on my finger. 'So … I guess you passed this mysterious test Dylan was going on about, then? You got the job?'

I looked down at the Ring of Privilege. 'Not yet. The ring came along a little bit early. I suppose I was just too annoying for the detective to keep holding out.' I smiled wryly. 'I'm going to meet with Arnold Albright now. And to be honest, I don't think I'll be getting the job once he's heard what I have to say.'

'Oh.' She looked disappointed. 'That's a pity. I have a good feeling about you. I really liked your hutzpah on the train – the way you argued with me was priceless. I told Dylan he should have let you help us out, actually.'

'Really?' I smiled. 'Well … he should have, the stubborn idiot. I guess I'd better head off. It was great to see you again, Gretel.'

She smiled warmly. 'You too. And Ash – I really *do* hope you stick around. It's about time they got some new blood over at the Daily Riddler.'

≈

I stood at the front gate of an elegant mansion. Large bay windows were looking out onto the street, and I was fairly sure Arnold already knew I was there. I checked my watch – five minutes late. Totally unlike me, but today was hardly a usual day.

I pulled myself together (and by that I mean I smoothed down my hair and tried desperately to stop my hands from shaking) and approached the front door. I pressed the doorbell, stood back, and waited.

Less than a second later, Arnold opened the door. 'Aisling,' he said, looking as nervous as I felt. 'Come in, come in. I have everything ready in the library.'

He was moving slowly, most of his weight supported on his cane. I followed him into a wide, high-ceilinged hallway, and on into a room to the right.

The wall next to the open double-doors was filled with brooms, sitting on holders and shined to perfection. One of those brooms was much simpler in its design than the others. The bristles looked older and messier, and the wood was crooked. But for all its flaws, it was the one I couldn't keep my eyes off.

A window occupied another wall, and the other two walls were filled with books. There was one of those library-style ladders I'd often dreamt of. It seemed like a necessity here, seeing as the books were stacked from floor to ceiling.

One of those books, though, had pride of place. It wasn't sitting on a shelf. It was atop a lectern, right in the middle of the room. The book itself was an enormous, leather-bound tome with symbols on its cover. Symbols that I felt like I *should* understand. I gazed at it, feeling an odd pull in its direction.

'I see you're a book lover,' Arnold said. 'That certainly bodes well.'

'Actually, I think hard copies are ridiculous in this day and age,' I said. Well, that was a big fat lie. Sure, I read mostly on an e-reader, but that was only because I spent my life terrified to accumulate too many belongings. I'd dreamt of a library like this ever since I was a kid.

And now that I was standing in the room of my dreams, I wanted to cry with happiness, because this space felt like home. I could picture myself as a kid, sitting in one of those enormous, over-stuffed armchairs, reading like a maniac with a cup of hot chocolate by my side.

I could picture what it would have been like to be here with a mother. Any mother. Just a mother. Maybe she would take me out on that crooked broom in the afternoon, and we'd fly to the shop to buy more books and hot chocolate.

'Oh,' he said. 'Well … I suppose I see what you mean. You can increase the font size on those new-fangled things, can't you? That could come in handy for old eyes like mine.'

I felt my nose twitch in irritation. The niceness was all for show, just like everything about him. If I wasn't the person he was looking for, he would push me straight from his mind and move onto the next person who fit the bill. 'Look, I'm going to be upfront with you, Mr Albright. I haven't come here to do your test.'

His eyes rounded. 'But … you must.'

'I *must*?' I cocked a brow. 'Mr Albright, I'm not your performing monkey. And I'm *not* doing this test. I don't want to know if I'm your granddaughter. I don't want to *be* your granddaughter.' A wave of exhaustion came over me, as the events of the past week finally caught up. I wanted to be back in the Vander Inn right now, curled up on that lovely bed with Fuzz. No matter how much I liked this library, I wanted to be anywhere but here. 'You need to hire a reporter, Mr Albright, and I've proven this week that I'm more than up to the job. So either hire me based on my work, or say goodbye to me forever.'

He gritted his teeth. 'This is all because of that simple-minded Dylan Quinn. He had no *right* to tell you what he told you. Because of him, you've had all this time to let silly thoughts fester. You're probably just nervous. You've spent the past nights worrying about what the test entails, no doubt. But I assure you – it's *nothing* to worry about. I know you're my granddaughter, Aisling, and it will only take a moment to prove it.'

I moved into his eye line, staring at him. 'You're not listening to me,' I said. 'Dylan did the *right* thing when he told me the truth. It's you who's in the wrong. But you seem to have a hard time accepting anyone's wishes other than your own, so I'll tell you again – I am *not* taking your test.'

He hobbled away from me, his hands shaking. 'You have to. I've told you already – you're the *only* candidate to have advanced this far.' He pointed to the book standing on the lectern, the leather-bound one that I'd felt drawn towards. 'That is our coven's grimoire. It can only be opened by Albright hands. The grimoire is the final test. All you have to do is open it. Then we'll know for sure.'

I ignored the pull I felt towards the book, and stood resolute. 'Firstly,' I said, 'if your daughter broke *her* daughter from the coven line, then what's to say that the book will even respond to that child?'

'Well, I … it's just one in a whole series of tests, though, don't you see? The final piece of the puzzle. You're a good reporter. Your writing is just like Abby's. You clearly have some degree of magic, even if it can't be seen through an Aurameter. This final test is just … it's just …'

'It's just impossible,' I said, shaking my head. 'I touch that book, and it doesn't open, and then what? Then your last sentences are proven to be a load of horse poop. You're saying it's just the final piece of the puzzle? The final hoop for me to somersault through? Yeah, right. All it is, is the thing that happens before you try and mess with my memories.' I stepped closer to him. 'And Arnold, *any* of those three women could have been your granddaughter. Any of them. You never let them get far enough to know. All of this time, you've just been prolonging your misery – and messing around with innocent people's lives in the process.'

I really did wish that my words would get through to him, but the expression of stubborn desperation didn't so much as falter on his face. I backed away, keeping an eye on him, hoping that he wouldn't do anything stupid.

'My decision is final, and you need to respect it,' I said, my voice wobbling.

I turned and walked towards the hallway, but I made it less than three steps before the doors slammed shut, locking me inside.

Panic rose in my chest, and I pulled at the door handles. They wouldn't budge an inch. Maybe this was it, at last. Maybe he was about to do his memory mojo. I forced myself to stop panicking, and turned to him with the most even of expressions I could muster.

Instead of a man hell-bent on messing with my mind, though, I found myself face-to-face with a man who seemed to have lost *his*.

He was standing before me, the coven grimoire in his hands and insanity in his eyes. 'I won't let you leave until you've touched the grimoire. I can't. I won't lose you, too.'

As he began to move closer, holding the book out, my eyes darted around the room, searching for a means of escape. The thought of being related to this man was even more terrifying than the thought of losing my memory. 'If this is how you treated your daughter,' I said, 'then no wonder she left.'

I had hoped to shame him into submission, but he kept coming at me, leaning on his cane with one hand and clutching the book with the other. There was no way I was going to touch that grimoire. My fear of him was growing by the second. What would happen if I *was* his granddaughter? I had visions of a life in a locked room, while Arnold insisted that he was just trying to keep me safe.

Before he could thrust the grimoire into my hands, I ducked and ran for the window, grabbing a heavy book from a shelf. If I threw it through the window, maybe someone would hear the racket and come to see if anything was wrong. And if they didn't, then I would crawl through that broken glass, and run for my life.

I hurled it with all my might, and then cried out in disappointment as the book bounced off the window and fell to the floor. I wanted to fall to the floor along with it, but I wasn't about to give up. If he thought he was going to force me to stay here, then I was going to show him *exactly* what life with me would be like.

I picked up another book and threw it – I knew it wouldn't break the window, I just wanted to make a very big mess. I threw more and more books, and then I grabbed ornaments, smashing them on the ground. I had just picked up one of the brooms, and I was holding it over my knee, about to snap it in two, when I heard Arnold say, 'Conáil.'

As soon as the word left his mouth, my body stilled.

'You … what have you done?' Even as I asked the question, I already knew the answer. Conáil was an Irish word for *freeze.* And that was just how I felt – frozen, immobile.

He gave me a look of wounded innocence. 'Forgive me,' he said. 'But I had to do it. You gave me no choice. It's just a simple freezing spell. A light one, too. You can still speak. And if you're a good girl, and promise to do as I say, then I'll ease it even more.'

I glared at him, more anger than I'd ever felt before welling up inside. I wasn't just angry at him. I was angry at my stream of foster families. Angry at the system. Angry at my mother. Angry at myself for daring to hope he would do the right thing.

As he strode towards me once again, I felt like that well of anger was expanding within me, taking on an energy of its own. It was growing, spreading all through me, until it felt so big I was afraid I wouldn't be able to keep it inside.

'No!' I screamed, the anger spilling into my words. 'I don't want to *be* your granddaughter. Stay away from me, Arnold. Stay away!'

As I screamed with all my might, his facial expression began to change. His stubbornness turned to surprise as his body was hurled back through the air. He landed against a bookshelf, a strange, dull thudding noise sounding all around him as the books fell to the ground.

And then … he just lay there. The anger inside me turned to dread as I stared at him, unable to move, unable to check if he was all right. 'Are … are you all right?' I asked. I had no idea what I'd done or how I'd done it. All I knew was that an old, frail man was lying on the ground, and I'd been the one to send him there. 'Please say you're all right.'

He let out a long, weary sigh. 'No,' he said. 'I'm not all right. But that's not your fault. The blame is all mine.'

I felt my body free up, and a clicking sound came from the door behind me. 'You're free to go,' he said. 'I won't make you do anything you don't want to, Aisling. All I ask … all I ask is that you forgive me.'

I hesitated for a moment. Thoughts and fears were rushing through my mind, banging into one another and creating a right ruckus. This could be his one last ploy. He could be pretending to be contrite just to get me to go over there and touch that stupid grimoire. But he didn't *look* like he was feigning anything. He just looked weary, sorry, and sad.

He sat up and nodded to the door. 'Well? What are you waiting for?' he said. 'Get out of here and leave me in peace.'

He was right. What *was* I waiting for? I pushed all doubts aside and ran for the door, dashing through the hallway, yanking the front door open and rushing out into Riddler's Cove.

I didn't stop running, not until my lungs screamed out and my legs grew weak. By then, I was almost at the market again. And it was at that moment, as I stood holding my chest and panting, that I realised: there was a broom right beside me, hanging in the air.

24. A Little Bit Witchy

There was no rider on the broom. It was just hovering there, next to me. And it wasn't just any old broom. It was a broom with a crooked shaft and uneven bristles. I reached out and, as my hand came in contact with the wood, a spark of electricity flew through me.

'You look like one of the brooms from the library,' I said, trying to minimise my shivers of excitement. 'Why are you here?'

The broom made a funny little judder, and I gasped. 'So … what's the plan, broom? You're just going to stay flying beside me, all the way back to the Vander Inn?'

There was another judder from the broom.

'Okay then. Do what you want to do. But you'd better be prepared, broom – because pretty soon, the deranged old guy who may or may not be my grandfather is going to come after me and try to get me to touch that book again. Which will lead to a fight. Which will lead to him doing some jiggery-pokery with my memory and sending me back to Dublin. And you can't come there with me. Because I live in a human enclave. A grotty flat in a human enclave, might I add. There's barely room to swing a cat. Not that I would. I have a feeling that Fuzz might swing me right back.'

I kept babbling away as I walked through the town and on into the Wandering Wood. Just like when I yammered to Fuzz, I felt sure the broom was listening.

By the time I arrived back at the Vander Inn, the evening poker crowd had arrived. I couldn't face that many people, so I kept my head down and made my way to my room.

My room. I sighed. It wasn't my room. It never had been. It was just a lovely dream that I'd enjoyed for a while. Arnold was sure to have gotten over his shock by now, and if his actions over the last thirty years were anything to go by, then he wasn't going to stay docile for long. He'd be speaking to Grace any minute now, telling her that I needed to touch the grimoire or get out of town.

And if that was the case, I really shouldn't be cut up about it. Sure, I'd met some people who I liked a lot. But there was also the small matter of the supernatural-on-supernatural hatred, the steady stream of murders, the local humans who were oblivious to the magic that was happening all around …

And then there was Detective Quinn. He was the grumpiest, rudest man I'd ever met. And I was including my old editor John in that assessment.

All in all, it might be good to get back to normality.

When I opened the door to the bedroom, the cat was sleeping on the bed. 'Hey Fuzz,' I said, scratching behind his ears. 'I won't bother asking if anyone let you in. Your ways and means can remain a secret. I don't think you'll be *too* surprised to hear that my meeting with Arnold didn't go all that well. I refused to touch the Albright coven grimoire and then sent him flying against the wall. So … I've had better job interviews.'

Fuzz purred, rubbing his head against me, sending a lovely wave of calmness my way.

'You're right,' I said. 'Things will work out the way they're meant to. You and me will stay together, somehow. No matter *what* Arnold does.'

He stopped purring suddenly. His ears pricked, and he turned to look at the open door. I followed his eyes there, watching as the broom flew right in and settled down on the bed beside the cat. Fuzz began to purr again, and then he rubbed his head against the bristles and lay down next to the broom. Well, of course he did. And of *course* I was convinced that the two were having a conversation while they lounged. Because … y'know … I was in the kind of town where anything was possible.

I was just about to check on the train timetable when my mobile phone began to ring. The number of the Daily Riddler flashed on the screen. You know that saying about your heart being in your mouth? Well, that was how I felt just then. Terror and hope intermingled, and I knew for certain: I wanted to stay here so badly that it hurt.

I swiped to answer. Before I had a chance to say a thing, Grace began to talk.

'I've just been speaking to Arnold,' she said. 'He told me you refused to take the test. Well, good for you. And I mean that sincerely, Ash, not sarcastically – though I'm aware that my tone sometimes fails to differentiate between the two. But I *am* sincere. I think you did the right thing. I like you, Ash. You're a good egg.'

I laughed softly. 'Well, that's nice, I guess. You might have to like me from a distance, though. Did he tell you what's going to happen now? I've been wondering whether he'll suddenly appear in the Vander Inn. And I can't just sit here, twiddling my thumbs and waiting for my memories to disappear. I think it might be best if I just get on the next train. Oh, and also – did he happen to mention a broom?'

There was a pause, and then Grace said, 'He did mention that one of Abby's brooms had decided to follow you home, and he told me you're welcome to keep it. He also said you and he parted on bad terms, but I thought he would have at *least* tried to make his position clear. You're not going anywhere, Ash. Well, unless you want to.'

I held the phone away from my face and prodded a finger about in my ear. I *had* to have heard her wrong. 'Come again?'

She let out an irritated tut. 'I mean, I've already had words with Arnold, but I'm going to have even *more* words with him as soon as I can. Ash, I don't know what you said to that silly man. All I know for sure is that you refused to take the test. But whatever happened between the two of you … well … it seems to have been the kick up the behind he needed. He wants you to stay on. Based on your journalistic merit, according to him. He says the choice is yours, but either way he won't try to interfere with your memory.'

'Oh,' I said. A moment later I added another, 'Oh.'

'Yes. Quite. Listen, I have to go now. But I hope I see you on Monday morning. Nine sharp. Oh – and I should probably tell you now while I think of it – I lied to you today. Your piece wasn't just satisfactory. It was wonderful.'

≈

It was Monday morning, and I sat in the dining room of the Vander Inn, chowing down on a big bowl of porridge and chatting with Pru. Nollaig and

Jared were up in bed, and there were no other guests.

Pru's breakfast was a red smoothie, and as she drank it my mind travelled back to the previous Monday morning, when I met Bathsheba on the train. Detective Quinn had assured me Donald would be treated leniently, and I hoped it was true. I already had a series of articles in mind that I intended to write if he went to trial. Public opinion mattered, and I knew that if enough people understood why Donald helped his wife to die, then a trial might go his way.

I felt positive about the outcome. I felt positive about everything, in fact. Outside, the sun was shining and the birds were singing, and I knew I was exactly where I ought to be.

Pru put on her sunglasses and smiled. 'I'm going to work up in Dublin today,' she said. 'There's a big fête taking place on the posh side of the city. Sometimes I feel like I'm stealing candy from a bunch of great big human babies, seeing as I can read their minds. But I figure, that's what any fortune teller does – right? We just tell people what they already know. Like last night when I told my brother that you wouldn't go out with him if he were the last man on earth.' She pulled her glasses down a touch and wiggled her eyebrows at me. 'Because you wouldn't. Would you?'

I shrugged, digging into my porridge. 'You've already told me you'd never stoop so low as to read *my* mind, so I guess you'll just have to figure that one out for yourself.'

'Speaking of unscrupulous vampires,' said Pru, 'I think I ought to teach you to block. My brother is not above fishing about in that lovely brain of yours – so he can pretend that you and he just *happen* to like all the same music and movies. I should warn you though, just like not all vampires can read human or witch minds, well … not all witches can block vampire intrusions. But we could give it a try.'

I laughed. 'You're forgetting something, Pru. I'm not a witch. I'm a … well … I don't know what I am.'

She didn't respond. She was too busy looking over my shoulder. I turned to see what was so interesting, and a bubble of happiness rose up inside.

It was Fuzz, arriving in the dining room – sitting right on top of the flying broom, no less. What did I tell you? Riddler's Edge was the sort of town where *anything* was possible.

Pru giggled and reached out to stroke the cat. 'Sure. You're not a witch, Ash. Tell you what? Why don't we just call you a little bit witchy for now?'

≈

You've reached the end of *A Little Bit Witchy.* I hope you enjoyed this read. If so, join my mailing list to keep up with the very latest releases: http://www.subscribepage.com/z4n0f4

Or visit: https://aaalbright.com and sign up there. On my website, you'll also find a list of my other available books – including my *Wayfair Witches* series, which is set in the same magical world.

Witchy See, Witchy Do is the second *Riddler's Edge* Mystery, and it's available now from Amazon.

If you'd like to find out a little more about Ireland's supernatural inhabitants, on the next page you'll find the latest *Extract from the Compendium of Supernatural Beings.*

Extract from the Compendium of Supernatural Beings

Edition 5002.
Year of Publication: the Year of the Woodpecker (otherwise known as 2018 AD).
Chronicler: Adeline A. Albright (Senior Chronicler and Librarian, Crooked College, Warren Lane, Dublin 2)

Major Supernatural Beings

Witches:

Witches, both male and female, are considered the most magical of supernatural beings. Their power is innate and (almost always) inherited. It would not be possible to list all witch abilities in this compendium, however many witches choose to specialize in one particular area. In the Year of the Lotus (2017 AD), Materialization was the most popular subject at Crooked College for the second year in a row. The Society for Senior Witches stated that this was 'proof that witches are sliding further and further towards the pits of hell.'

Most witches belong to covens. Whilst each family may legally form a coven of its own, it is more usual for the smaller, newer witch families to join the covens of the larger, more established families.

Due to increasing pressure from other supernatural factions in recent years, witches have recently made their enclaves accessible to all other supernaturals. Whilst all supernatural enclaves (sub-dimensional regions) have always been accessible to witches, until recently the witches have kept their own enclaves closed to all but a privileged few.

During the Winter Solstice of the Year of the Lotus, Agatha Wayfair, the now deceased Acting Minister for Magical Law, issued updated versions of the Pendant of Privilege to all Irish supernaturals. The old (and some would say ugly) jewellery was redesigned, and there is now a choice of rings, necklaces and other jewellery which will grant the wearer access to the witch enclaves.

Warlocks:

The warlock movement has been around for centuries. It began in the Year of the Snout (2001 BC), when a small group of male witches formed the Warlock Society. Their original manifesto has been lost to the ages, but it is widely accepted that their modern manifesto is representative of the society's early beliefs: that men are unfairly represented within the matriarchal structure of witch society, and recognition of their unique male capabilities is important to society as a whole.

Warlocks are (genetically speaking) witches. They'd just rather not be reminded of that fact.

Wizards:

(Note: This edition of the Compendium is only the second to include wizards in the Major Supernatural Beings section. To find references to wizards in compendia prior to the Year of the Lotus, the chronicler suggests you begin looking under the section labelled: Others)

Wizards can be male, female, or anything else they like. They are also known as mages, shamans and wiccans, and are often overlooked. This is due to the fact that wizards are almost always of human origin. Their power is neither innate, nor inherited. A wizard's power is hard won and, because of that, deserves the utmost respect.

In February of the Year of the Woodpecker, wizards were finally granted equal rights, and they now have access to all major magical enclaves, tomes and educational facilities. Considering how far their power advanced without these privileges, this chronicler predicts an interesting future for wizards. Already, wizards are expert at harnessing and directing the elements, and utilising OUPs (objects of unusual power), OAPs (objects of awesome power), AUPs (areas of unusual power) and AAPs (areas of awesome power). With their new legal rights, they are sure to progress further.

Wizards traditionally reside in the human enclaves, most often working in science and technology – though a small few run candle stores, yoga studios, holistic centres and the like. In recent years, witches have – somewhat – relaxed their attitude to wizards. They have been free to work in witch enclaves for a number of years, but now they are also free to reside there. As yet, very few wizards have made the move, preferring to remain in the enclaves that have always been open to *others*.

As of December in the Year of the Lotus, there were more wizards working in the magical devices sector than there were witches. Sales of wizard-made brooms have now surpassed witch-made brooms.

Mages: See entry for Wizards

Shamans: See entry for Wizards

Wiccans: See entry for Wizards

Werewolves:

Werewolves are an example to us all that, with the right attitude, you can make a curse work *for* you. There are many conflicting chronicles of how, when and why these beings were hexed. Werewolves themselves have a long-standing policy of neither confirming nor denying any single chronicle.

What we do know is this: during the full moon (and including the day preceding and the day following said moon) all werewolves transform from their humanoid body, becoming wolves for three consecutive nights. Over the course of these three nights, the change begins at sunset and ends at sunrise. Because of this, the transformation tends not to affect werewolves in their daily lives.

The werewolf curse can be passed on via a simple bite or scratch to any part of the body. The curse has many upsides: unusual strength, longevity (some werewolves have been known to live as long as vampires) and good looks. Rigorous testing has proved that even the ugliest human or witch, when transformed into a werewolf, instantly becomes more attractive.

The lure of werewolf-hood is irresistible to many witches. The well-known actress Veronica Berry has recently been turned by her werewolf lover, lead guitarist with the Call of the Wild. In a statement to *Young Witch Weekly,* Veronica said, ‘I was warned that I could lose quite a large chunk of my power, but that didn’t happen. I’m just as powerful as ever – except now I get to frolic with my gorgeous lover during the full moon.’

Before she turned, there was much speculation that Veronica – already considered an incredibly beautiful witch – would become the best-looking witch in history. Opinions are mixed on whether Veronica has achieved that aim.

Vampires:

Like the werewolf curse, there are many conflicting chronicles of the origins of vampirism. Many vampires have submitted themselves for testing, and recent findings confirm that vampirism is, indeed, a blood-borne virus – albeit a virus with extremely unusual behaviour. The blood of a vampire is both a poison and an antidote.

Often a human will resist a vampire bite. This is, frankly, the most foolish thing they could do. A willing *bitee* (as the vampires refer to them) will be drained by only a minor amount. Full penetration of the vein will do no damage whatsoever, and may even give the *bitee* a burst of energy equal to a strong cup of coffee or a shot of ginseng. After the bite, the vampire will perform a simple act of hypnotism, thus striking the event from the *bitee's* memory and leaving them with nothing but a spring in their step.

If the human resists and manages to escape before full penetration, a vampire bite can leave the victim feeling weak for days. Often, humans will complain of flu-like symptoms.

The process of becoming a vampire is a little more complicated than becoming a werewolf: in order to turn, you must drink a vampire's blood before sunset on the day following the original bite. It is always preferable to drink from the vampire who administered the bite. Drinking from a different vampire can result in many complications (further details of which can be found in the Compendium of Supernatural Ailments). In recent years, the virus known as Dayturning was thought to be caused by such turnings. New evidence, however, suggests that either the original assessment was wrong, or the Dayturning virus is mutating. For further information, see *Dayturner* entry.

Benefits of the vampire virus are numerous. They include: increased strength; near-perfect health (a small number of humans and witches with terminal illnesses resort to vampirism in order to cure their illness. In the majority of cases, the vampire virus does, indeed, provide a cure); ability to transform into a bat; ability to transform into a nearly-invisible vapour; ability to hypnotise; telepathy (the telepathic link can generally be established from vampire to vampire only, however there are some vampires who can read the minds of all creatures); long lifespan.

Problems associated with the vampire virus include: blood-drinking as the main source of nutrition (a small subset of vampires who were vegetarian in their previous life have set up the No Food with a Face Foundation. They are currently researching many alternatives to blood. Promising results have been seen with a vitamin popular in the human world, known as B12); sensitivity to daylight (although the hat and sunglasses sector is quite happy about this); long lifespan.

Dayturners:
(Note: in compendia published prior to the Year of the Lotus, dayturners were listed in the *Others* section)

A hitherto rare being, dayturners are becoming more and more common, with three hundred new dayturners registered in the Year of the Lotus. Dayturners are vampires who feel the need to feed by daylight, and are incredibly sensitive to the dark. Feeding at night leaves them with serious indigestion (often resulting in hospitalisation). Additionally, venturing outside after sunset results in a rapidly spread rash, for which there is no known cure.

The original assessment of the disease concluded that the virus was activated primarily by careless turning practices (drinking from a vampire other than the one who administered the bite). More recent research has, however, concluded that there are other ways of contracting the virus. The virus is becoming more communicable by the day, and *any* bite from a dayturner, no matter what precautions have been taken, should be avoided. Even long term, standard vampires have been affected by the dayturner virus in recent months, as tainted blood has begun to make its way onto the market. It is imperative that vampires verify the origin of their blood before consuming.

A number of private and charitable organisations are spearheading the search for a cure, and government-run research (which was suspended in the Year of the Lizard – 2016 AD) is expected to resume in the near future.

Weredogs:

(Note: in compendia published prior to the Year of the Lotus, weredogs were listed in the *Others* section)

Like werewolves, the shifting of a human into a dog is controlled by the full moon, but instead of transforming into a supernatural version of *Canis Lupus Lupus,* they transform into any of the many breeds of *Canis Lupus Familiaris*. There is little known about the origin of the species. In the Year of the Cat (2010 AD), outspoken vampire politician Mildred Valentine claimed to have been sent evidence that the weredogs are descendants of werewolves, having come about as the result of long-ago trysts between werewolves and *Canis Lupus Familiaris*. Both werewolves and weredogs hotly deny this. However, neither side will agree to DNA testing. As for the evidence Mildred Valentine allegedly received? She has refused to produce it, stating that doing so would endanger her source.

Familiars:

Familiars are animals with limited magical capabilities. They usually reside with witches. A witch does not choose her familiar. The familiar chooses the witch. The most common familiar animals are cats, though other animals have been known. The most notable magical ability of a familiar is the ability to communicate in any language it chooses – thus, familiars may communicate freely with their witches. They *have* been known to converse with other supernatural beings, but only when they want to. Speaking with humans is rarer still for familiars, but not unheard of.

The Unempowered:

Not to be confused with the disempowered, the unempowered witch is, like the wizards, far too often overlooked. In fact, unempowered is a modern term, and will not be found in compendia earlier than the Year of the Cat (2010 AD). Before then, there was no word for these witches. Officially, they did not exist. In the compendia dating from the Year of the Cat to the Year of the Lizard (2010-2016 AD) you will find the unempowered under the listing: Others.

In rare cases, a witch is empowered from the moment of conception, but most do not display any signs of power until a little later (five or six is the norm). The very latest that any witch has been known to come into their power is twenty-one. If they have not been empowered by then, they never will.

Some unempowered witches study wizardry, in order to gain power by other means. In the Year of the Lotus, twenty-eight percent of new enrolments at Wentforth's College for Wizards were unempowered witches. This was a fifteen percent increase on the year before.

Like all supernaturals other than witches themselves, unempowered witches must wear special jewellery in order to access witch enclaves.

Although recent changes in Magical Law have meant that unempowered witches now have equal rights, many unempowered still choose to live outside the witch enclaves.

The Disempowered:

A disempowered witch is a witch who has been stripped of all power, as a result of crimes committed. This can only occur by decree of the Wyrd Court. The length of disempowerment depends on the crime in question. In serious cases, a witch may be disempowered for life.

Books by A.A. Albright

All of my books are set in the same magical world, with the same magical rules and supernaturals occurring throughout. Each series itself is self-contained, and you don't need to read any one series to understand another. But my characters do reserve the right to pop in on one another from time to time to make a little cameo or two.

Books in the Riddler's Edge Series:
Book One: A Little Bit Witchy
Book Two: Witchy See, Witchy Do
Book Three: Lucky Witches
Book Four: Shiver Me Witches
Book Five: So Very Unfae
Book Six: Old-School Witch
Book Seven: A Little Bit Vampy
Slippery Slope: A standalone featuring Pru, with the action occurring between books seven and eight of the main series
Book Eight: A Little Bit Chilly
Book Nine (Coming in Autumn 2020): A Little Bit Spacey

Riddler's Edge Standalones:
Slippery Slope: A standalone featuring Pru, which can be read on its own – if you'd like to read in order with the main series, the action occurs between books seven and eight

Books in the Wayfair Witches Series:

Book One: Bottling It
Book Two: Bricking It
Book Three: A Trick for a Treat
Book Four: Winging It
Book Five: Wrapping Up
Book Six: Loved Up
Book Seven: Rocking Out
Book Eight: Acting Up
Legally Red: A standalone featuring Melissa, with the action occurring between books eight and nine of the main series
Book Nine: Swotting Up
Book Ten: Forget Me Knot
Book Eleven: All Hallowed Out
Holiday Heist: A standalone featuring Melissa, with the action occurring between books eleven and twelve of the main series
Book Twelve: Doing Time (Coming in late 2020)

Wayfair Witches Side Stories:

(These books can be read as standalones, but if you'd like to read them in order with the main series, see the list above for their placement in the series timeline)

Legally Red
Holiday Heist

Books in the Katy Kramer Series:

Book One: The Case of the Wayward Witch
Book Two: The Case of the Haunted House
Book Three: The Case of the Listening Library
Book Four: The Case of the Strange Society

Boxed Sets:
Riddler's Edge Books 1-3
Wayfair Witches Books 1-3

Made in the USA
Las Vegas, NV
26 March 2022

46362745R10152